"Is that why you came back?"

Josh leaned on the wall facing her. His angry dark eyes were fixed on her as he continued. "Did you want to cause the maximum amount of damage to everyone who hurt your mother?"

"I don't think like that!" Prue retorted. "You may be cold-blooded enough to go looking for revenge, but I'm not."

"Oh, I wouldn't dream of suggesting you're cold-blooded," Josh said, smiling in a way that made Prue uneasy. "Although after watching you with your fiancé today, I did wonder...does he know?"

"K-know?" she stammered, bewildered by the question.

"That your emotions were locked up in a deep freeze years ago and that you don't know the first thing about loving anyone."

CHARLOTTE LAMB began to write "because it was one job I could do without having to leave the children." Now writing is her profession. She has had more than forty Harlequin novels published since 1978. "I love to write," she explains, "and it comes very easily to me." She and her family live in a beautiful old home on the Isle of Man, between England and Ireland. Charlotte spends eight hours a day working at her typewriter—and enjoys every minute of it.

Books by Charlotte Lamb

Don't miss any of our special offers. Write to us at the following address for information on our newest releases.

Harlequin Reader Service
901 Fuhrmann Blvd., P.O. Box 1397, Buffalo, NY 14240
Canadian address: P.O. Box 603,
Fort Erie, Ont. L2A 5X3

CHARLOTTE LAMB

seductive stranger

Harlequin Books

TORONTO • NEW YORK • LONDON
AMSTERDAM • PARIS • SYDNEY • HAMBURG
STOCKHOLM • ATHENS • TOKYO • MILAN

Harlequin Presents first edition January 1990
ISBN 0-373-11236-X

Original hardcover edition published in 1989
by Mills & Boon Limited

CHAPTER ONE

'YOU'RE quiet,' David said, but Prue was staring out at the stormy landscape, her green eyes bleak, and didn't hear him. They were almost there—and she was getting cold feet. Maybe she should have told David all about it, but that would have seemed disloyal while her mother was alive—and, oddly, more so since her mother's death six months ago.

David waved a hand in front of her face. 'Hey, are you in there?'

'Sorry! I was thinking,' she said, smiling an apology. When they were planning this trip to Europe, she had said that she would like to visit Yorkshire to see her father, and David had agreed without asking a string of questions. It was typical of him; he wasn't curious or interested in the past. The present was all that mattered, he said; and that was just one of the reasons why she loved him. He was easy-going and casual; he didn't brood or cling to grievances as her mother always had.

'How much further?' he asked. 'I seem to have been driving for ever.'

'Just a couple of miles away now.'

'You're right—two miles to Hallows Cross!' said David, looking at a signpost they were passing. 'Weird name!'

'It's a euphemism, actually!' Prue said with sudden

amusement.

'It's a what?'

'The village was originally called Gallows Cross . . .'

'Don't tell me! There used to be a gallows at the crossroads!'

'Yes, but in Victorian times, people hated to be reminded about that, so they changed the name.'

'Oh, it's that sort of place, is it?' David grimaced, and she laughed.

They both spoke with an Australian lilt, although Prue had only lived in Australia for ten years, while David had been born there. His native sun had given him golden skin to match his golden hair; hours on the beach, surfing, swimming and sailing his sleek little yacht had given him a lithe, athletic body. Prue sighed; Australia seemed very far away. She had begun to miss it as soon as they left. It had been spring there; her favourite time of the year. They had arrived in England to find a wet and windy autumn; on the Yorkshire hills and moors the heather was purple, the gorse still yellow, although the bracken was already turning russet and bronze, a colour less vivid than the flame-red hair which blew around her face in the wind from the open car window.

This was a landscape of contrasting colours: gentle, misty, blue and grey-green distances, mysterious wooded valleys and softly rounded hills on which grazed ambling sheep. Prue had not seen this countryside since she was thirteen years old, yet it was so familiar that it hurt, like a blow over the heart. She kept catching her breath; a sense of uneasiness was growing stronger the closer they came to her old home, although she couldn't pin down any sound reason for feeling anxious. It must be pure nerves. She had no idea what to expect when they did arrive.

'Penny for your thoughts,' said David, and she started, eyes wide.

'They're not worth it.'

'I can read your face, you know!' he said softly, putting a hand on hers. 'Are you wishing you hadn't come, Prue?' His blue eyes stared down into her green ones, and she shrugged ruefully, unsurprised by his intuition. They had known each other a long time and David knew her very well. He leaned over to kiss her. 'Don't worry, it will be OK, just relax and take things as they come.' It was his motto for life, and she couldn't help laughing.

He grinned back, and at that instant they came over the crest of the hill, and almost ran smack into another car coming from the opposite direction. It was all so sudden that Prue hardly knew what was happening. Dazedly, she saw a red car flash by, horn blaring, tyres screaming.

Prue stared, open-mouth, at the startled face behind the steering wheel, a hard face from which wild, black hair blew back.

David instinctively swerved sideways. The other man had already shot over to the righthand side of the road, and they might have avoided an accident, but in his panic David lost control, or perhaps the brakes failed. Whatever the reason, still going much too fast, the car smashed into a stone wall with a noise of crumpling metal and splintering glass.

Prue had her seat-belt on; she was flung back and forth like a rag doll, hitting first the door and then the windscreen, her long, red hair thrown across her face, blinding her. She ended up sprawled forward in her seat in a state of shock, and for a moment was barely conscious, until she remembered David and sat up, white-faced. He lay very still over the wheel; broken glass glittering in his hair, blood crawling down the side of his face.

'David!' she groaned, white-faced, unbuckling her seat-belt with hands that trembled, but, before she could scramble over to him, the door beside her was wrenched open, somone grabbed her by the waist and dragged her backwards out of the car.

Startled, Prue struggled, looking round into the grim, dark face of the other driver. She had had the barest glimpse of him as they passed, but that face was burnt into her brain. She was sure she would never forget it.

'Never mind me, I'm OK, get David out; I think he's badly hurt,' she gabbled, trying to push him away, quite uselessly since he took no notice, and was too strong for her, anyway. He lifted her out of the car and carried her, kicking and protesting, to a safe distance.

'Put me down! I can walk; will you please get David out?' she yelled, and he deposited her abruptly on the rough, heathery bank which scratched her legs and hands. She gave a cry of pain which he ignored, striding back to the car. Prue watched fixedly as he lifted one of David's hands by the wrist. She knew he was looking for David's pulse, and her stomach clenched in sick anxiety. His face told her nothing, and after a moment he let go of the hand, but he didn't try to pull David to safety. Instead, he began prowling around the car, peering into the engine.

'Never mind the car!' Prue burst out, and, still a little dizzy began trying to get to her feet. 'What the hell are you doing?' She was so angry that her voice wavered, and that got her a searching glance from dark, impassive eyes.

'Sit down before you fall down!' he ordered, and she bristled.

'Why don't you get David out of there?'

'He's unconscious,' he coolly said. 'And it could be dangerous to move him until we know how badly he's injured.'

'But it's dangerous to leave him in the car! What if it explodes?'

'There's no smell of petrol. What do you think I was doing? I was checking on the petrol tank; it isn't damaged, although the bonnet has buckled. The engine seems OK. I can't see any leakage of fuel, and I don't think . . .'

'Damn the car! What about David?' Her green eyes blazed in her strained white face and his eyes narrowed, observing her, but his voice was still very calm.

'His pulse seemed regular.'

'But he's unconscious! I'm no doctor, but I think we ought to get him to a hospital as soon as we can—we have to get to a phone! Will you stop wasting precious time, and drive to the nearest telephone box?'

'I've already rung the local hospital. An ambulance should be here any minute.'

She stared at him blankly. 'You've rung the

hospital? But . . . but how?'

'I have a phone in my car,' he said casually.

That possibility hadn't occurred to her. 'Oh! Oh, yes, of course!' she said on a thick sigh of relief.

'Now, will you please just sit and be quiet!' he commanded, turning around to check on David again.

She was still feeling very shaky so she obeyed him, her whole body slack and icy with shock, but she stared at his back view with dislike. He had a very high-handed way of talking—giving orders as if he had a right to lay down the law to everyone! She disliked everything about him, yet she still couldn't help feeling she had seen him before somewhere, or maybe that she had heard that voice before! A distinct sense of *déjà vu* kept recurring whenever she heard those clipped, insistent go-to-blazes English tones.

Maybe he lived in the district? She could have met him at any time during her childhood, of course, but it couldn't have been very frequently or she would have a definite memory of him. She remembered quite a few of the local people. Or was she simply remembering voices like his? Was his face familiar? Her green eyes ran over him assessingly: tall, with long legs and slim hips, that black hair, a sharp-etched profile, nose long, mouth hard and controlled. He wasn't handsome, but he was physically compelling, He was tough, and much too sure of himself.

That thought made her frown again. It had reminded her of something, but just as she had almost tracked the memory down she heard David stir. She looked quickly at him; his hand was moving.

He lifted it to his head, as if in pain, then gave a faint groan.

'How do you feel?' the other man asked him, bending down, and Prue forced herself to get up. She must go to David, reassure him. It would be worrying for him to open his eyes after being unconscious, and see a total stranger looking down at him. He would wonder what on earth was going on!

'What happened?' he was whispering, his voice so low she only just heard it.

'You were in an accident, but don't worry, you aren't badly hurt.'

'Oh . . .' David's voice faded, then he said hoarsely, 'I remember now . . . Prue . . . where's Prue?'

'I'm here,' she said, shakily covering the short distance to the car, but David had closed his eyes again by the time she got there. While she was looking down at him she heard the ambulance racing towards them. She swayed on her feet, deathly cold suddenly, and the dark man put an arm around her, holding her up.

'I told you not to move!' he said, and she eyed him with disfavour.

'It must be nice to know you're always right!'

He smiled faintly. 'Are you always this aggressive? Or is this just the way you cope with shock?'

The ambulance pulled up nearby and men raced towards them. One of them went immediately to David; the other came over to Prue and the other man.

'Hello, Phil,' he calmly said, and the ambulance-man gave him an unsurprised nod, smiling in a friendly way.

'They told us it was you who rang in, Josh! We passed your car back there; it looked as if it was OK. What happened?'

'That guy came over the hill half-way over my side of the road. We both swerved, and I pulled out of it easily enough, not a scratch on either me or my car, but as I was driving on I heard him crash, I reversed until I could see what had happened, rang the emergency services, parked and ran for help.'

'Superman!' Prue said bitterly, and they both looked at her.

The ambulance driver laughed. The other man didn't.

'She was in the car with him,' he said coolly. 'Better take a look at her, Phil. She seems pretty shocked.'

The ambulance driver became very professional; a moment later Prue was in the ambulance, on a stretcher, covered with a blanket, and it was only as the warmth of it got through to her that she realised how cold she was, how her body was shaking. They carried David into the ambulance, and she sat up on her elbow to watch, but he had his eyes shut and they were quickly setting up a blood transfusion. Prue bit her lip anxiously—how badly was he hurt? They wouldn't be giving him blood if he hadn't lost a lot. The only injury she had noticed until then had been the one to his head, but now she saw blood on his shirt and her heart skipped a beat.

'Is he badly hurt?' she asked one of men, and they soothingly said no, he wasn't, but she didn't believe them. The door shut, one of the men stayed beside David, doing something to him. She couldn't see—his back hid David from her—but she was afraid and tears began to run silently down her face.

What if he died? What on earth could she say to his mother and father, who had always been so kind to her, especially since her own mother died? She had brought David over here to Europe! She had talked him into coming up to Yorkshire when he would probably have been much happier staying in London or going over to Paris, as they had planned to do next week. David wouldn't be here if it weren't for her—and she would understand if his family blamed her for this accident! She blamed herself.

When they reached the hospital they were taken to the Casualty department for a while. Prue was seen briefly by a doctor, who seemed satisfied with a quick examination but would not answer her questions about David. After about half an hour she was wheeled away to a female ward, and put to bed.

'Listen,' she said to the nurse looking after her, 'where have they taken David, my friend . . . the man brought in with me . . .? I want to know what's wrong with him, I want to see him.'

'He's gone straight to theatre,' the nurse said, and Prue drew a sharp breath, her eyes frightened.

The girl noticed her expression and smiled comfortingly. 'But don't worry, he's in good hands, and I don't think he's badly injured at all. He's only having a pretty straightforward op. In a couple of hours he'll be tucked up in the ward next door—male surgical—and when you're up on your feet you'll be able to see how he is for yourself!'

'How long will that be?'

The girl looked confused. 'Sorry?'

'Before I'm back on my feet.'

Hesitantly, the nurse said, 'Well, that's not for me to say, it's up to Dr Wilson, but not too long, I imagine.'

'I'm not hurt,' protested Prue. 'A few bruises and cuts, that's all.'

'I wouldn't know, I just work here,' the girl grinned. 'Look, you've got a visitor—can he come in now?'

'A visitor?' Prue was suddenly flushed, and angry with herself for this instant reaction. It had to be that man, of course! In all the flurry of being admitted to hospital she had forgotten about him, and she wished she could go on forgetting. Why had he come? He had been efficient and cool-headed, and she knew she ought to be grateful to him, but something about the man had put her back up.

'Well? Shall I let him in?' the nurse demanded, looking at her with a curious smile, and Prue pulled herself together.

'OK,' she said reluctantly, and the nurse left her. Prue leaned back on the pillows, watching the swing doors of the ward. Why should he come? He had known she wasn't badly hurt, and he couldn't have felt responsible for the accident; his blistering comments on David's driving had made that clear. He surely couldn't have thought she would want him to visit her! He must have realised she was in love with David, even if he hadn't noticed her engagement ring.

Of course, he might have come out of courtesy, or kindness! Prue made a face. She was being very ungrateful, wasn't she? She ought to thank him, not resent him. She owed him that much—and that reminded her! She must make a phone call as soon as possible. She would ask her visitor to help arrange it. It had slipped her mind until now, but she and David were expected, and if they didn't arrive . . .

Her nerves jumped as the ward door swung open, but it wasn't the dark-eyed man who walked towards her, it was a much older man, of a very different type. His thick, reddish hair had turned silvery, his weather-browned skin was lined, he had a faint stoop to shoulders that she remembered as broad and strong—but she knew him at once, in spite of the ten years since they had met.

'Prunella,' he said huskily, standing beside the bed and looking awkward and unsure of himself, and his voice sent a shiver down her spine because that, at least, hadn't altered. She would know that voice anywhere.

'Hello, Dad,' she whispered, stupidly holding out her hand as if expecting him to shake it.

He laughed gruffly and took her hand between both of his, sat down suddenly on the bed and leaned forward to kiss her cheek. 'Prue, Prue,' he said, his cheek against hers, and she had an uneasy suspicion he was almost crying. 'You look so grown-up.'

'I am grown-up,' she said, trying to laugh, but just as much on edge. She hadn't known how she would feel when they met again. Her emotions towards her father were so complex: a cat's cradle of anger and pain, love and guilt, too inextricably entwined to be unwound. She hadn't even been sure if it was wise to come, or whether she should leave him in the past along with all those sad childhood memories. She had been sure only that she wanted to return to

Europe for a visit; a holiday would help her to get over the grief of her mother's death, and she felt a yearning for the landscape of her childhood, for those happy far-off years when everything had seemed so safe and unchanging.

She had had to put the trip off for a while, because there was so much to do first. She had sold the furniture, along with the house, and she had worked out a month's notice at the office in Sydney where she'd worked. She had good friends there; she would probably go back on her return to Australia, unless David chose to live elsewhere after their marriage.

'I was sorry to hear about your mother. It's hard to believe she's dead,' Jim Allardyce said.

'It's hard for me to believe it, too!' she admitted, trying to merge this tired, sad man with the father she remembered.

'It must have been a shock for you, and you had to cope all on your own! You should have cabled me—I'd have come right away.'

'I had lots of good friends to help me, and Mother . . .' Her voice cut out as she realised that she couldn't end that sentence; nor did she need to, surely? He must know that her mother wouldn't have wanted him, of all people, at her funeral?

He flinched, as if she had struck him, and she felt guilty again. She knew nothing about his life today, except that he hadn't married that woman who had wrecked his marriage. Her mother had sneered over that. 'Well, she wouldn't want that, would she? They would both have been ruined,' she had said tartly. She, herself, had remarried; Harry Grant had been a good man, Prue had liked him, and her mother should have been happy, but she had nursed her bitterness and resentment to the end.

'I wrote to you, but you never replied,' Jim Allardyce said. 'Oh, I don't blame you for not answering, Prue, but I wondered . . . did she let you see my letters?'

'Now and then,' she said; but the truth was, her mother had usually suppressed them, and hadn't let her reply. Prue had realised she was being used as a weapon against her father, but there had not been much she could do about it. Her mother had begun to cry if she mentioned him, so she had gradually let his memory fade, then after her mother's death she had found all those faded old letters, hidden in the back of a drawer, and she had been torn between wanting to see her father again, and dreading it. Why dredge up the past? she had argued with herself, but she had come.

'I didn't even recognise your writing!' her father suddenly said, and she looked at him searchingly—had he felt the same muddle of emotion when he got that letter, saying she was coming? Was he, too, still not sure how he really felt?

'Well, it is a long time.' She smiled shakily at him. 'And this isn't how I planned to meet you again, either!'

He laughed at that, relaxing. 'The best laid plans of mice and men? Maybe it's a blessing in disguise. I was feeling very nervous, waiting at the house for you, listening for the sound of a car. I was already in a state of shock when I heard about your accident.'

'I'm sorry,' she said, liking this familiar stranger

whom she had to get to know all over again. 'It's a
pity somebody jumped the gun. It would have been
better if I could have told you myself; that way you
wouldn't have had such a shock. At least you would
have known I was OK! When you arrived, I was just
thinking that I ought to ring and reassure you before
you started calling in bloodhounds to search for me
on the moor!' She gave him a wavering grin, then
added, 'When we first arrived, the receptionist asked
me for my next of kin, and I gave your name and
address, so I suppose they let you know?'

He hesitated. 'No, it wasn't the hospital,' he said,
looking uneasy, and her curiosity was aroused.

'Then how did you hear?' she firmly persisted.
Why should he be reluctant to tell her that?

'It was Josh,' he said, his eyes sliding away, and
she had a brief, painfully vivid memory of that
expression on his face when he and her mother were
having one of their bitter rows. Even when she was a
very small girl, Prue had known that her father
would do anything to avoid conflict. That look would
come into his face; he would be evasive, try to change
the subject, escape from the room if he could. He was
not an aggressive or dynamic man, Jim Allardyce. He
was gentle—and she had loved his gentleness—but
he was also a stubborn man with the unexpected
obstinacy of the weak. He had hated the arguments
and tension, but he would never give in, especially
where the farm was concerned. Before her mother
had decided there was another woman, their rows
had always begun with the farm, the life it compelled
them to live, the lonely emptiness of the landscape in
which he lived and worked so happily, but which her

mother had hated. Her mother had had so many grievances; she was that sort of woman: sullen, suspicious, jealous.

But why was he looking like that now? 'Josh?' she repeated. Who on earth was Josh? Then she remembered, her eyes widening. Wasn't that what the ambulance driver had called the dark man? 'Josh? Is that the man David nearly drove into?' She watched her father's nod. 'You know him?' Her father nodded again, and that surprised her at first, which was stupid, because this was a small community; everyone knew everyone else. She remembered that much, all the gossip and curiosity—it had caused some of the trouble between her parents.

'How is David?' asked her father. 'He's your fiancé, isn't he?'

'Yes, I told you about him in my letter. We're over here to look at Europe for a few weeks—a last big fling before we get married and settle down.' Her face sobered. 'The nurses keep saying he's going to be fine, but you know what hospitals are like—could you find out the truth? They might be frank with you.'

'I'll do my best,' her father said gently, holding her hand in a firm grip, and she looked down, biting her lower lip. There was silence for a moment; she heard the grave tick of the clock on the wall, an unhurried and remorseless sound.

Prue looked up, remembering something, and blurted out, 'But how did he know who I was?'

Her father stared blankly. 'What?'

'That man, Josh—how did he know who I was? I

don't remember telling him my name or that I was coming to visit you.'

After a pause, her father said flatly, 'He recognised you.'

'How could he? We hadn't met before.' This time her father didn't answer, his head bent, and Prue stared at him. She was thinking hard. 'Or have we?' she said slowly. 'I don't remember, if we have.' Yet she had had an odd, puzzling sense of familiarity, hadn't she, from the first? It had confused her, disturbed her, because she had mistaken it for something else. A slow, hot flush crawled up her face as she admitted to herself what she had thought was bothering her. Well, at least she had been wrong about that!

'You sent me a photograph,' her father reminded her. 'With your letter saying you were coming back to England. I've got it on my desk and Josh saw it.'

She felt a jolt of surprise, almost of disappointment. 'Oh, I see.' So it was that simple; nothing mysterious or odd or suspicious, after all! But why, in that case, had her father been so uneasy, so reluctant to talk about it?

'Do you remember my office, at the farm?' James Allardyce had a rueful look in his eyes. 'Do you remember the farm, come to that? It must all seem very dim and distant to you after ten years.'

'Some of it,' she agreed. 'But I remember a lot, too, although I expect my memory was selective—it usually is, isn't it? I remember my bedroom and the swing under the apple tree, and the hay loft, and the stables . . . the places I liked, in other words.' She smiled at him. 'I hope they aren't going to keep me in here for too long!'

'I talked to the doctor before I came in here—you should be allowed home tomorrow.'

Home, she thought, biting her inner lip. The word had a poignant ring; he used it casually but she couldn't accept it that way—the farm was no longer her home, it hadn't been her home for a great many years.

'Has it changed much?' she asked, and James Allardyce laughed, shaking his head.

'I wouldn't say it had changed at all.' The thought seemed to please him, and Prue felt a stab of satisfaction, too. She wasn't sorry to hear that the places and things she remembered hadn't altered much, and yet shouldn't they have changed in ten years? Everything did; why not the farm?

'You still run sheep?'

'The land's too acid to support anything else. Very thin soil, too; there isn't enough grass for cows. Sheep do pretty well on the hills. Mine are more like goats than sheep; climb anywhere. We don't have the sort of sheep territory they have in Australia, our flocks don't roam so far, and they're smaller.' He hesitated, then wistfully asked, 'I don't suppose you saw anything of sheep farming while you were in Australia?'

She smiled ruefully. 'I worked in an office in Sydney, I'm afraid. All I saw of pasture land was when I once spent a school holiday, visiting a friend whose father was a farmer.'

'Well, farming is a boring subject, I suppose,' her father said on a sigh.

'But I'm very interested!' she protested.

His face brightened. 'Are you? Are you really? You aren't just saying that?'

'Of course not—why shouldn't I be interested? Tell me about your flock—how many sheep have you got?'

Jim Allardyce didn't need a second invitation. Prue settled back on her pillows and listened, watching her father and remembering him as he had been the last time they met. He had changed a great deal; and yet she was recognising more and more the father she had known when she was a child. They had once been very close; she had loved both her parents and it had been a blinding shock to her when her mother had left, taking her too. Prue had realised that her parents were always quarrelling, but she hadn't expected them to separate for good.

Her mother had blamed her father; she hadn't hidden any secrets from Prue, she had wanted her to know why they were going away, and had talked endlessly, bitterly, about the break-up of the marriage. Prue had been entering her teens; gawky, shy, unsure of herself. The next couple of years had been miserable for her. She had to cope with a new school, new friends, a new country, new home—and a mother who had nobody else to cling to, needed constant sympathy, and was over-possessive.

Prue had been hurt and angry, too—not because her father had preferred another woman to her mother, but because he hadn't tried to stop her mother taking her away. Then Susan Allardyce met another man, and both their lives changed again, this time for the better. Prue had been very fond of her stepfather, who had been a nice man, but Harry

Grant was more than nice—by taking the burden of her mother on his shoulders, he had freed Prue to live her own life. She had settled down at school, made friends, discovered the freedom of the sun and sea, and pushed all thought of England and her father to the furthest corner of her memory, until the car crash in which Harry and her mother had been killed.

The nurse reappeared, scolding. 'Still here, Mr Allardyce? I told you ten minutes, and you've been here half an hour or more! Off you go, now! You can come and pick your daughter up tomorrow morning at ten.'

'How's her fiancé?' Jim Allardyce asked, getting to his feet.

'He's doing fine,' the nurse said in just the same tone she had used to Prue. 'Now, come along, Mr Allardyce.'

'Anything I can get you, Prue?' he asked, lingering, and Prue shook her head, smiling at him.

'I'll see you tomorrow, then,' he said, leaving, but it wasn't her father who came next morning at ten o'clock to pick her up. Prue was up and dressed, waiting by the window, looking out over the windswept moorland behind the hospital. She saw the red car drive up and park, and stiffened incredulously. The dark head moved below her across the forecourt to the entrance, and her eyes followed it. Was he here to see her? Or was it a coincidence that he was visiting the hospital today?

A moment later he walked into the ward and she heard the muted stir of curiosity among the other patients; everyone stared, whispered.

'I'm here to collect you,' he said, picking up her suitcase from the end of her bed. 'Your father got caught up in an emergency; some of his ewes escaped on to the main road, and he had to round them up before someone ran them down. As I was coming into town, I said I'd pick you up.'

She gave him a tight little smile. 'Thank you.' He was being kind again, and she ought to be grateful, but why did he always talk to her in that go-to-blazes voice? I've come to collect you, he said, as if she was a parcel, and all the time those jet-black eyes of his were wandering over her in a desultory fashion, making her both uneasy and furious.

'But I'm in a hurry,' he said, striding off, and Prue had to run to keep up with him, pausing only to wave a last goodbye to the other patients.

In the corridor they met the ward sister, who said briskly, 'Off now, Miss Allardyce? I expect we'll see you when you visit your fiancé.'

'Could I see him now?' Prue pleaded.

'He's asleep at the moment; we don't want to wake him, do we?'

'No, of course not,' Prue sighed. 'When can I visit him, then?'

'I should let him rest today; he's under sedation. Come tomorrow afternoon. Visiting hours are from three to four o'clock.' Her pale eyes then flicked to the man carrying Prue's suitcase, and she gave one of her rare, slightly chilly smiles.

'Good morning, Mr Killane, nice to see you.'

He gave her a nod. 'Hello, Sister Wood.'

Prue froze on the spot; her green eyes wide and shocked. Killane? He was a Killane? Josh, she thought in a slow, stupid way. Josh Killane—of course she remembered him, not that she had seen him very often. He had moved in a very different world from hers, but he had ridden over her father's land with the local hunt. She remembered him very well; he had been mesmeric with that black hair and those dark eyes, in the drama of his red coat, buff breeches and knee-length black leather boots. Prue had watched the hunt from her bedroom window, but she had never ridden with them. She had a pony, like most of the farmers' children in that part of the world, a shaggy moorland pony bought cheaply at a horse auction and broken for her by her father. It was a stolid, patient, gentle creature, but her mother wouldn't let her hunt, and anyway, Prue had been divided in her loyalties. She loved foxes, and hated the savagery of the hunt, yet the huntsmen on their tall, sleek horses had such glamour, particularly Josh Killane, who was a superb horseman, and usually leading the rest of the hunt across hedges and over fields, riding as if he was part of the horse, arrogantly, gracefully, carelessly.

Most of the land in the valley belonged to the Killane family. They owned several farms as well as the one they farmed themselves. They had lived at Killane House since the Napoleonic wars when a returning soldier bought up a great stretch of land, built himself a solid, elegantly functional house, planted a park around it, and started a dynasty.

Her father was one of their tenants; he had been born on the farm which his father had then rented, and he loved the place. Her mother had been a Londoner; she had hated the Killanes and what she called the feudal way of life in the valley. After she married James Allardyce, she tried to get him to leave his farm, go to Australia, where she had a brother, but he would never listen. At first, she had believed him when he said he simply couldn't bear to leave Yorkshire, but gradually she had come to believe that he had another reason for staying in the valley, among the Killanes.

Josh Killane's mother, Lucy, had been the other woman who had wrecked that marriage and driven Susan Allardyce and Prue away to Australia.

CHAPTER TWO

PRUE was so engrossed that she was barely aware of
walking out of the hospital, getting into the car,
driving away. Josh Killane drove capably; Prue
noticed that at last, if reluctantly, prickling with
hostility. He didn't seem aware of her; his profile
razor-edged, eyes fixed ahead. He was wearing
casual, working clothes: blue denims, a blue shirt, a
sheepskin jacket. He still looked tough and he still
had the same glamour. It wasn't just the aura of
power, or money; the man himself was somehow
compelling.

She disliked his manner, his self-assurance, his
way of talking, looking at her, but she had to admit
that he was not someone you could ever overlook.
His features were too masculine; all angles and very
insistent. She had a vague idea that he took after his
father in feature, as far as she remembered Henry
Killane—but in colouring he undoubtedly took after
his mother. She could see Lucy Killane now, if she
closed her eyes, so she did, and immediately
summoned up the elegant, beautiful woman who
had haunted her childhood. Was she still alive? Did
she still have that sleek black hair, the eyes of
gleaming jet, the flawless camellia skin?

'Why have you come back?' Josh asked abruptly,
and she opened her eyes wide at the tone of his voice.

'To see my father!'

'After ten years of silence, you suddenly remembered him?' His voice was dry with sarcasm and she flushed with anger.

'I'm not discussing my private life with you, Mr Killane!'

'I'm sure you don't want to, but you're going to have to . . .' He paused, then emphasised her name, 'Miss Allardyce!'

'Oh, no, I'm not!' Prue said through her teeth. 'You know nothing about me . . .'

'I know your father wrote to you for years without getting a single reply!' he said bitingly. 'Oh, I'm sure he won't reproach you. He's too happy to have you back home to say anything. I'm not going to let you get away that easily, though!'

'This is none of your business!'

'I'm making it my business!' His voice had a harsh rasp, but Prue wasn't backing down, however much he glared.

'Now, look!' she burst out, but he just raised his voice several decibels.

'I like and admire your father and I know how much it hurt him, all these years, having a daughter on the other side of the world who wouldn't even send him a Christmas card!'

'Don't you shout at me!' seethed Prue, tempted to hit him with something. 'Things are never as simple as they may look to an outsider, and that's what you are, Mr Killane—an outsider! You only know one part of the story, my father's, and I'm ready to bet you don't even know his for certain. I think you're guessing at what he feels. You certainly know nothing about what was going on in my mind—or my life, come to that—over the last ten years. You don't know what you're talking about, so until you know something more about me, will you please . . .' She drew breath, fighting with her temper, then it got away from her and she snapped, 'Butt out, Mr Killane!'

He had slowed and was staring at her, his face hard. A lorry snarled passed them and that pulled his attention back to the road. He accelerated again, his eyes on the cars coming towards them, and didn't say anything much for a while, then he said coolly, 'You may see me as an outsider, but I doubt if your father would. I've known him all my life, remember; he's not just one of our tenants, he's an old family friend.'

The flush on her cheeks deepened. Was he hinting at the long affair between her father and his mother? Or was he blind to the truth? She had asked her mother how the Killane family felt, and her mother had laughed bitterly. They were too stupid to see what went on right under their noses, she had said, but could they really have been?

'Is your m . . . Are your parents still alive?' she asked him, sliding a sideways look at him, her lashes down over her green eyes. His face hadn't changed; she could see no uneasiness or awareness in those hard features. If he knew, wouldn't he betray it somehow?

'My mother is,' he said. 'My father died just over four years ago.'

So his mother had been a widow for over four years? Prue frowned. Yet Mrs Killane and her father had not got married once she was free? Was their affair over? Prue thought of the way her father had looked yesterday: grey and a little weary, beginning to show his age. He had still been a very attractive man ten years ago, it had been easy to believe that Mrs Killane might love him, but now he was definitely middle-aged; after all, he was well past fifty. Had their feelings for each other burnt out or faded away with time?

Of course, she couldn't ask Josh Killane any of these questions. She had just told him to wait until he knew more about her before coming to any conclusions; the same advice applied to her. If her father and Mrs Killane were still emotionally involved, she wasn't likely to miss it when she saw them together. People couldn't hide their feelings. Her green eyes were wry. Or could they? If the Killane family hadn't noticed anything going on all those years, maybe the lovers were good at hide and seek!

It was all academic now, anyway! Her mother was dead; and it couldn't matter to her now whether or not she had been right in her suspicions.

Prue's mouth tightened. It matters to me, though! she thought. I want to know, for my mother's sake. I want to know if she was imagining things all those years, if she was just a neurotic with a suspicious mind—or if she was cleverer than anyone else around here. It's time I knew the whole truth, and I owe it to her to find out, if I can.

'There's the farm,' Josh Killane said, and she glanced upward automatically, without realising for a moment that she had remembered exactly where the farmhouse stood on the hillside they were climbing.

'It hasn't changed,' she said huskily.

'Things don't, around here,' Josh Killane said with satisfaction.

For some reason that made her laugh, a little jaggedly, and he looked at her, narrow-eyed.

'What's funny about that?'

'I don't know,' she muttered. 'Nothing, I suppose! You just sounded so pleased about it!'

'Why shouldn't I be?' he asked with faint aggression.

Prue didn't answer for a moment, her green eyes roving around the hills and sky, the autumnal trees, the fainly misty valley.

Her mother would have been appalled to hear that nothing in this valley had changed; she had hated it here! But Prue was glad to find the landscape, the farmhouse, everything she had seen on this drive from the hospital, so deeply familiar. The world changed fast; events rushed people onwards as if they were riding a whirlwind. While she was making her plans to come home, she had often warned herself to expect changes. In ten years this part of England could have been altered beyond recognition, and she felt amazingly comforted to find that it had not.

She looked round at Josh Killane. 'As it happens, I'm rather glad too,' she ruefully admitted. 'I was afraid I wouldn't recognise anything, it would all be different, and I badly wanted it to be just the way I remembered it.'

He grimaced, his dark eyes wry. 'Oh, I wouldn't

hope for that—what you've been remembering may not be what you really knew. We tend to idealise what we've left behind.'

She looked at the tussocky heather, the gorse, the almost leafless thorn trees on the hillside they were climbing. It was hardly an idyllic landscape; indeed, it was rough and forbidding, a landscape of survival rather than one of rich fertility, such as she and David had seen down south, on their way here.

Yet this countryside had its own beauty, one to which her heart instinctively responded. This was where she had first opened her eyes, and she saw beauty where a stranger might not.

'Oh, I don't think I've idealised anything,' she said, smiling, and Josh Killane smiled back at her, a spontaneous smile, full of warmth and charm.

'Welcome home, then,' he said, and she felt a strange leap of the heart.

They had reached the summit of the hill. Josh Killane suddenly pulled up at the side of the road, turning towards her, still smiling, an arm sliding along the back of the seat. Prue stiffened, her face uneasy, her intuition working overtime. He wasn't going to make a pass, was he? Did he think one smile was all it took?

'Why have you stopped here?' she demanded, body tense.

He stared for a second, then his lids half veiled his dark eyes, and his mouth curved in a crooked smile. 'Why do you think?'

That did it. Prue was sure she wasn't imagining anything; the silky tone of voice or that mocking little smile. 'Will you start this car again, please?' she snapped, reaching for the door-handle, ready to leap out if he got any closer.

'Oh, not yet,' he said, lazily putting out one hand, but instead of touching her face he flicked the windswept red hair back from her averted profile, so that he could see her better.

'Keep your hands to yourself!'

'There's no need to work yourself into a tizzy,' he drawled, grinning. 'I didn't park here to make a grab at you, so you can stop breathing hard and shaking in your shoes!'

'I'm not doing either!' she said at once, furious, but he looked smilingly unconvinced.

'Aren't you? Then you're doing a great imitation of a female in a panic, and I can't think why you should. I only stopped here so that you could see the view!'

Prue stared, open-mouthed. 'The view? Who do you think you're kidding? I wasn't born yesterday.'

'No? And I was beginning to think that could be the only explanation!'

She gave him a green-eyed glare. 'Aren't you funny?'

He eyed her without so much amusement then. 'Miss Allardyce, I'm beginning to feel that for some reason you don't like me.'

'Whatever makes you think that?' she sweetly asked.

His mouth set hard. 'Get out of the car!' he said brusquely, and she tensed at the way he said it.

He leaned over her as he finished speaking; his body touched hers briefly, but there was no provocative intention behind the contact. His dark eyes when she stared into them were hostile, not sensual. He opened her door and Prue almost fell out. Unsteadily, she turned and walked over to the drystone wall, so typical of the walls up here in the north of England; often built centuries ago to mark off land boundaries or keep sheep from straying, miles and miles of straight or meandering grey stone walls, in summer often overgrown with grass and gorse, in winter more prominent, like wintry veins across the barren fields. In dry weather, the walls were a dusty grey, but in rain they took on new life and shimmered, a slaty blue-black. She put her hands on the roughness of the stone, felt an insect tickle her skin, pressed down a soft cushion of lichen which left a yellow powder on her finger, but she was only half aware of doing anything; she wasn't even really looking at the stunning view below. She was brooding angrily over what had just happened.

She might have over-reacted when he stopped the car here without warning—but he had had some fun at her expense and she didn't like it!

He got out of the car, too, and came up behind her. 'If you look over the wall, you'll be able to see the whole valley from one end to the other,' he said coolly. 'It's a better view from here than you'll get from your father's farm, and I thought it might help you get your bearings again, jog your memory a little.'

She stared down over the hillside to the valley far below; running in a misty green-grey sweep between the rounded hills. She could see the slate-roofed little market town and the hospital on its outskirts, from where they had just come; the main road and little toy-like cars moving on it, the village of Hallows

Cross at the foot of this hill; a spire, a huddle of grey roofs and flinty walls, the village green in the centre by the church.

'I didn't need my memory jogged,' she said. 'I hadn't forgotten anything.'

'Except me?'

A funny little shiver ran down her spine and she was glad she had her back to him because she wasn't sure what he might read in her face.

'I didn't really know you,' she said stiffly.

'Didn't you?' he murmured, and that icy shiver hit her again. What did he mean by that?

'I don't think we so much as shook hands!' she snapped; suspecting another of his deliberate teases.

'We kissed, though!' he said, but when she swung round, eyes wide open and incredulous, he was walking towards the car, saying over his shoulder, 'We'd better get on to High Hallows before your father sends out a search party!'

Prue climbed back into her seat, slamming the door to relieve her feelings. Obviously, it was nonsense. They had never kissed—for heaven's sake, she had only been thirteen when she left here, and Josh Killane had been . . . how much older? Ten years? More like twelve, she thought, eyeing him secretly. He must be thirty-five now.

She decided not to argue with him, though. She was beginning to realise he was mischievous; the more she reacted, the more he provoked her. The best way of dealing with someone like that was to take no notice of them. Let him play his little games! She would ignore him.

A half-forgotten quotation drifted through her head

as they drove on up the road. 'He only does it to annoy because he knows it teases.' She couldn't remember where it came from, but it summed up Josh Killane! He was, after all, his mother's son; and hadn't her own mother always said that Lucy Killane was a born flirt and an inveterate mischief-maker? Prue had often doubted her mother's judgement about the other woman, not because of anything she herself remembered about Lucy Killane, but because of what she knew about her mother's jealousy and capacity to hate. Maybe she owed her mother an apology?

She forgot all that though as Josh slowed the car to turn in between the open gates of High Hallows Farm. A high, mossy stone wall ran along beside the road, hiding the house from the view of casual passers-by. Josh drove up the narrow drive between banks of untidy laurel and rhododendron bushes above which stooped bare whitethorn trees, their branches creaking and moaning in the wind. The house appeared and disappeared as they drove; an old house, square-built, of greyish stone, with a slate roof, a well-weathered oak front door with a great iron ring set in it for a doorknocker, wind-blistered white and green paint on the window-frames, and a look of endurance as it faced the onset of another winter.

Josh pulled up and Prue got out of the car, staring up at the house, remembering.

Her father appeared from around the corner of the house. He was wearing an old tweed jacket, his trousers tucked into muddy wellingtons, an old tweed cap on his head. 'Has it changed much?' he asked as he joined her.

'Not at all,' she said, and couldn't stop herself giving Josh Killane a glance, but he apparently wasn't listening. He hadn't even got out of the car. He still had the engine running, and nodded to her father in a friendly way.

'I'm in a hurry, Jim. See you.'

'Hang on, Josh—Lynsey's here!' her father said hurriedly as the car began to move again, and Josh braked, a black frown dragging his brows together.

'What?'

'Josh, don't be too tough on her,' James Allardyce said softly, standing beside the car and lowering his voice so that Prue only just heard what he was saying. 'She's very young and she's finding it hard to cope.'

'It won't make it any easier if she keeps running away! And why come to you?' There was a grimness to that question, a resentment, which made Prue turn away. This was obviously a very private matter they were discussing and she shouldn't be eavesdropping, but she couldn't help wondering—who were they talking about?

As she walked towards the oak front door she saw a girl standing on the threshold; a girl in jeans and a T-shirt—very ordinary, everyday clothes for someone whose beauty made Prue stop and stare. Was this the girl her father was talking about? She couldn't be much more than twenty, but her bone structure was so perfect that, if she had been sixty, Prue suspected she would still be lovely.

'So there you are!' Josh muttered, grabbing the girl, and hustling her towards the car.

'Don't push me around, Josh!' the girl burst out, fighting him all the way. 'I've had enough, I can't take any more!'

'Snap!' he said, pushing her into his car in spite of her struggles.

'Josh!' protested James Allardyce unhappily, trying to intervene, but he was ignored. Josh slammed the door on the girl, strode round, got back behind the wheel and started the engine. A moment later the car shot away, making a racing noise and grinding up the gravel on the drive. Prue and her father stared after it in silence, then James Allardyce sighed.

'Oh, dear. I didn't handle that very well, did I? I promised Lynsey I'd try to make him see her point of view, but I didn't get the chance. Josh can be a difficult customer.'

'Not can be—is,' said Prue rather blankly, for some reason taken aback by the way Josh Killane had acted towards the other girl. Was she his girlfriend? She couldn't be his wife, could she? Prue hadn't looked for a ring on the girl's finger; she hadn't even thought of that until now, but for some reason she hadn't pictured Josh Killane as a married man. He certainly didn't act like one! Or, did he? Married men could flirt, after all, couldn't they? Some men didn't let a little thing like marriage stop them chasing other women.

Her eyes flickered to her father, a frown crossing her face. Her mother had always suspected him of chasing other women—one of them, at least. But had he? Prue simply didn't see him as the type, but how could she be sure?

'He can be formidable!' James Allardyce grimaced,

watching her troubled face. 'Is something wrong, Prue? Was Josh offhand with you? He isn't still furious over the accident, is he? But he can't blame you—your fiancé was driving, not you! I'm sorry I couldn't pick you up myself, but . . .'

'I know, he explained—wandering sheep!' She wound a hand through his arm, leaning on him. 'I understood. I'd have done the same in your place.'

He looked surprised, staring down at her. 'Would you?'

'I know I'm my mother's daughter, but I'm also yours, Dad—don't forget that!' She smiled reassuringly, and he put an arm around her, hugging her.

'I won't! Now, come and see your room. I've put you in your old room—I wonder if you'll remember it?'

'Of course I will. I remember everything,' she said, following him into the stone hall. The floor had highly polished red tiling; there was a fireplace big enough for a child to stand up in, in which she remembered hiding. On either side of it, in alcoves, were wooden benches and above them dark oak bookshelves. She stood there, inhaling the remembered scent of lavender polish, beeswax, flowers.

Her father went ahead, carrying her case up the winding, creaking stair leading to the first floor. She followed slowly, and now it was a sound she remembered. How many times as a child had she lain in bed and listened for the creak of her father's footsteps on the stairs? Farmers went to bed early, rose early—that was something else her mother had hated about the life here.

James Allardyce put her suitcase down and Prue stood in the doorway, looking around her at the dark-beamed ceiling, the neat little bed with a pink satin quilt and a pile of crisp white pillows, the polished oak floorboards on which home-made tufted mats were scattered, the chintz curtains sprinkled with apple-blossom print. She recognised it all; even the dressing-table fittings were the same.

'Nothing has changed!' she said wonderingly, and her father smiled at her, then his face changed, a sadness in his smile.

'A lot of things have changed, I'm afraid. You, for instance—you're all grown up, not my little girl any more . . . and your mother . . .' His voice broke off, he turned and looked out of the window, his back to her. After a moment he said, 'I'm so happy to have you back here, Prue. I don't wish your fiancé any harm, I'm sure I'll like him very much, but I'm not sorry to have you to myself for a while instead of having to share you with him.'

He didn't wait for Prue to answer, he swung round and made for the door before she could get out a word. 'Why don't you take your time to get used to the place again? If you need me, I'll be in my office.'

It was a peaceful day from then on; Prue unpacked and settled into her old room, then went downstairs and wandered around the house and garden, revisiting her childhood and feeling disorientated—yet quietly happy.

Her father found her sitting on the old swing under the apple tree, a sheepdog beside her. Looking up at the sound of his footsteps, Prue asked, 'This isn't old Bess, is it, Dad? She hasn't changed a hair.'

He grimaced. 'Bess died years ago, I'm afraid—that's her duaghter, Meg.'

'Oh, poor old Bess,' Prue said, saddened. 'So, you're Meg, are you? I knew your mother, long ago.'

James Allardyce watched her ruffling the dog's black and white ears. Smiling, he said, 'I came out to tell you lunch was ready.'

'You didn't cook it yourself?' Prue stood up, looking stricken. 'I meant to help you, not make more work for you to do!'

'I would have had to get myself lunch, anyway. Cooking for two is no harder.' Her father smiled at her. 'In fact, it's easier, because it is more fun! Eating alone gets to be a bore.'

Prue wondered if he had been very lonely all these years. Why hadn't she written? She had just pushed him out of her mind, hadn't she? Did he resent that? she wondered, following him back into the house, but although she watched her father secretly she saw no signs of either resentment or reproach.

Next morning she rang the hospital, only to be told that David still couldn't have visitors. He had developed a slight fever; nothing to worry about, the ward sister reassured Prue, but it would be safer if he was kept in isolation.

She spent the day getting to know her father better, walking around the farm with him and renewing acquaintance with their rough-pastured, hilly land and the surrounding countryside, being told about the sheep her father owned and watching the hoodie crows and the rooks, the magpies and hawks, all circling around the wandering flock, waiting their chance at them.

Her father watched the ominous skies, eyes angry. 'Damn birds of prey! Look at them up there!'

'Let's go home, and I'll make dinner tonight!' Prue comforted, and her father looked self-conscious.

'Tonight we've been invited to dinner at Killane House!'

Prue stood very still. Who had invited them—Josh Killane, or his mother? She felt the chill of a wintry wind blowing across the moors, lifting her red hair and striking through her clothes.

'Or would you rather not go out tonight?' her father asked.

She certainly didn't want to see Josh again; she had seen far too much of him already. She didn't want to see Lucy Killane, either. If she saw the two of them together, she might know how her father felt about Mrs Killane and she was no longer sure she wanted to know.

'That's up to you, Dad,' she said huskily.

He hesitated, watching her with a frown. Was he wondering how much she knew? He hadn't breathed a word about the cause of the separation between her mother and himself; did he suppose she had not been told about him and Mrs Killane? 'Well, let's see how you feel, shall we?' he said uncertainly. 'After all, you only came out of hospital yesterday.'

She knew that there was nothing wrong with her—the shock of the accident had worn off and her bruises were beginning to fade already. She didn't say as much, though. She seized on the excuse with relief.

'An early night might be wiser,' she murmured.

'And I just hope that my cooking won't give you indigestion!'

Her father laughed. 'No mock modesty, Prue! Your mother was a very good cook when she chose—I'm sure she taught you to cook!'

'She did,' Prue admitted, sobering as they turned back towards the house. She found it odd that her father mentioned her mother so often; and so unselfconsciously, almost as though she was an old friend he hadn't seen for years, but remembered fondly. Did he often think of her? Had he missed her when she went? Had he loved her, after all? Prue was curious, but knew she couldn't ask those questions. Her parents were a mystery to her, but no more so than any other human being; everyone was mysterious in their own way. She gave a faint sigh—she was a mystery to herself, come to that! She still wasn't sure how she felt about anything!

Her father looked at his watch. 'Look at the time . . . I must rush. I have a lot to do this afternoon. Prue, are you sure you want to cook dinner tonight? I don't feel right about letting you, you still look peaky to me. I can cook the meal, love, I'm used to doing it.'

'I'd like to!' she insisted. 'I'll take a look through the freezer and the larder, shall I, and see what I can find?'

'Aye, lass,' James Allardyce said reluctantly. 'If you've a mind! But after that, why don't you lie down for a couple of hours? I'll be back as soon as I've finished my work, and we can cook the dinner together!'

She smiled, nodding. 'OK, Dad. We'll do it together. It will be more fun that way.'

He went off looking very cheerful, and she looked at the larder and worked out what to cook for dinner, then she went upstairs and lay down on her bed, intending only to rest for half an hour. Instead she fell asleep almost at once, utterly exhausted by the day out in the fresh, windy Yorkshire air.

A sound awoke her; a click which, even half-asleep, she recognised as the click of her bedroom door. Someone had come into her room. Prue surfaced drowsily, but before she opened her eyes the door softly closed again. The stairs creaked and she slowly sat up, yawning.

'Dad?' she called. The creaking stopped; nobody answered, yet she felt someone out there, listening, breathing quietly, and her sleepiness vanished.

'Dad, is that you?' she called again, but still there was no answer. She began to be frightened, especially when the creaking began again. It was quieter this time, though; someone was moving very carefully, trying not to make a sound. She felt the emptiness of the house all around her, pressing down on her like a great weight. If that wasn't her father, who was it, and why didn't he answer?

She swung her legs off the bed and stood up, the hair on the back of her neck prickling with atavistic dread. Tiptoeing to the door, she suddenly pulled it open. The stairs were shadowy; it was late afternoon and the autumn dusk was falling fast, but she still saw the dark shape half-way down the stairs, a man whose elongated, black shadow ran up the wall until it touched the ceiling like something out of a silent horror film.

Prue froze, staring downwards, her heart beating suffocatingly fast.

CHAPTER THREE

THEN he turned his head to look back at her, the menace of his shadow fled, she recognised his face and the spell broke, but Prue did not merely feel a wave of relief! As her fear subsided, rage welled up inside her.

'What the hell do you think you're doing, creeping about the house like that?' she yelled, and Josh Killane swung round and began to come back upstairs again.

'I wasn't creeping about! I was moving quietly, that's all, trying not to wake you up!'

'How considerate,' she muttered. 'A pity you already had, creeping into my room, isn't it? And while we're on that subject, what were you after in my bedroom?'

'I wasn't after you, anyway, so you needn't have palpitations!' he said drily, and she got angrier, although in the beginning she had been more angry with herself—for imagining night-time terrors, conjuring them out of such small things—a creak on the stair, a shadow on a wall. She had been an idiot and she could kick herself, but she wasn't going to let Josh Killane make fun of her.

'You really fancy yourself, don't you?'

'Me, fancy myself?' He laughed without amusement. 'I'd say it was the other way round. This is the second time you've accused me of making a pass. Well, I wasn't making a pass the first time and I'm not now! You obviously think you're irresistible to the opposite sex, but I've got news for you—not to me, you're not. I can resist you without any trouble whatever.'

Prue showed him her teeth, dying to smack his face, but deciding that she wouldn't give him the satisfaction of hitting her back—as he undoubtedly would. He was the type.

'I notice you still haven't told me what you were doing in my room.'

'I was looking for your father, not you!'

Prue looked coldly incredulous. 'Looking for him in my bedroom?' she queried with icy sweetness.

'I called from the hall, but nobody answered, then I saw Meg lying on the landing outside the door,' he said with angry insistence. 'And I thought your father must be up here. I came up and looked into the room—and saw you on the bed, asleep, so I left as quietly as I could.'

Prue looked down at the dog which was still there; no longer lying down, though. Meg was standing close to her, conscious of the tension in the air, her dark eyes intent.

'I didn't know she was there! My father must have left her to take care of me!' She was touched by the idea; had her father come back to the house, seen that she was asleep and decided to leave her in Meg's protection?

'She's a good guard dog,' said Josh, watching her run a hand over the dog's black and white head. Meg looked up at her enquiringly, ears alert, as if waiting for a command.

'Good girl,' Prue murmured, patting her, but frowned. 'Why didn't she bark when you arrived, though? Isn't that what she was supposed to do?'

'She's known me all her life, she knows I'm always here—but if you told her to attack me, she would,' Josh said with bland amusement.

'Would she?' Prue considered the liquid eyes and adoring stance of the dog. 'Is she trained to attack?'

'No, but she's trained to obey, and her master left her to defend you, so if she thought you needed defence against me, she'd attack me.'

'Don't tempt me!' sighed Prue, half smiling, and got a grimace from him.

'I thought we'd established that that was the last thing on my mind?'

'Well, what a relief!' Prue said, half irritated by his mocking voice, 'Don't let me keep you! You'll find my father working—I'm not sure where. Take Meg with you, she'll find him.'

He shook his head. 'She wouldn't come with me.'

'Oh, she doesn't like you, either? A dog with taste, obviously!'

He went on smiling, his white teeth showing. 'She won't leave you until your father says so. She's a one-man dog.'

'Bitch, to be precise!'

'Oh, let's be precise—a one-man bitch,' Josh said, looking at her with angry black eyes. 'Quite a phenomenon.'

From the kitchen, at that moment, they heard the slam of a door, and Prue said quickly, with relief, 'My father!'

Josh turned on his heel and vanished down the stairs, and she went back into her room and stood by the window staring out at the thickening dusk. Her reactions to Josh Killane were odd; whenever she saw him she felt angry and belligerent, and that wasn't how she ever was with other men—with David, for instance! She was never aggressive with David.

Josh had a violent chemical effect on her. She couldn't deny that there was a sexual element involved; why bother to lie to herself? She didn't like the man, but she couldn't help being aware of him—on a purely physical level. It wasn't attraction, she hurriedly told herself. Far from it! She wasn't attracted by that overpowering masculinity; that was what made her want to slap him, yet something inside her reacted explosively to something in him, although she hadn't yet worked out what happened to make her feel this way whenever she saw him.

She stood at the window, brooding, until she saw Josh and her father come out of the house. They stood talking on the drive, beside Josh's red car, and Prue watched them. She would have had to be blind and stupid not to see the affection between them, the casual trust and friendship. Her father liked Josh Killane, even if she didn't, but then, her father was another man, he judged Josh by very different standards.

Josh drove away and Prue turned from the window and went into the bathroom to freshen up before going downstairs. She found her father in the kitchen; the kettle singing on the stove and cups laid out on the table. He looked round to smile at her.

'Had a good sleep? A pity Josh woke you up.'

'It doesn't matter. I'd slept long enough.'

Jim Allardyce poured the boiling water on to the tea in the fat-bellied, yellow earthenware pot. 'You seem to have more colour, anyway!'

Prue's flush deepened; she was glad he had his back to her. 'Thank you for leaving Meg to guard me,' she said, sitting down at the table. Of course, Meg hadn't barked at Josh Killane; Meg was another of his fans!

Her father joined her, covering the teapot with a hand-knitted tea-cosy. 'Meg's a good watchdog, inside and out.'

He offered her a plate of small, home-made biscuits. 'Try one of these; they're very good. Betty Cain made them. She works in the house three mornings a week. You'll meet her tomorrow.'

Prue gingerly tasted one while her father watched. 'Very good,' she said, taking another, and he grinned in satisfaction.

The situation was so ordinary—a family taking tea in a kitchen—yet she felt like someone trying to walk on eggshells. It was important that she and her father get to know each other again, learn to like each other! But what should have been a gradual, everyday thing had become an uphill struggle. Was it too late for them to get to know one another?

'Prue . . .' he said, in an uncertain voice, glancing at her while she poured the tea. 'About having dinner at Killane House . . .'

His eyes pleaded, and Prue resented that, for her mother's sake. Couldn't he spend one evening away from Lucy Killane? Or was he hoping that she and Mrs Killane would become friends? Whatever the truth, one thing was blatantly obvious—her father badly wanted to have dinner at Killane House that evening.

'Was that why Josh Killane was here?' she asked flatly. 'Did his mother send him to make sure we were coming?'

James Allardyce looked at her, then away, a dark flush in his face. 'No, he was here on estate business—we're wall-mending, before lambing starts, and Josh was making out the rota. We all help out on jobs like that; every year some walls get damaged by weather, both rain and snow can make a wall collapse, not to mention the sheep! It's a never-ending chore, like painting the Forth Bridge.'

'So he didn't ask if we were going there for dinner?'

Her father didn't look up. 'He mentioned it. I'd promised to let them know, and I'd been putting it off until you woke up.' He gave her another of those pleading looks, and Prue suppressed a sigh. How could she refuse when he looked at her like that?

'Well, if you want to go,' she said, and her father's face brightened.

'You'll come? I'm sure you'd enjoy it, Prue. It's a lovely house, you know—do you remember it?'

'Oh, yes,' she said with faint irony as he got up, but he seemed deaf to her tone, and suddenly in a tearing hurry to get to the phone.

'Lucy will be delighted,' he happily said. 'I'd better ring her now. Josh said he'd shot some partridges and Lucy will want to know how many birds she'll need to prepare.' He looked back at Prue. 'You do like partridge?'

'I can't remember ever eating them, but I like duck and quail, so I probably like partridge; one game bird is much like another, isn't it?'

He made a laughing face. 'I wouldn't say that, but I'm sure you ate partridge as a child; there are so many game birds on the estate and I used to bring them all home. I don't remember you disliking any of them. Crab, now, you didn't like that.'

'Seafood brings me out in a rash!' she said, moved that he remembered.

He picked up the phone on the other side of the kitchen. Prue drank her tea, frowning. She still wasn't eager to face Lucy Killane, but she had to meet her again some time—why not tonight? Every time her father mentioned the other woman her antennae quivered. Maybe her mother hadn't exaggerated or invented anything! She didn't know what was between her father and Lucy Killane—but she was sure there was something!

She listened to her father talking. 'Lucy? Jim. We're coming! Yes. Josh told me; Prue likes partridge, at least, we think she does!' His voice was warm, intimate, casual—and that was the real give-away. He was talking to Lucy Killane the way a man talks to his wife, and again Prue thought . . . if they love each other, why haven't they got married? There was no point in speculating, though, so she slipped upstairs to look through her wardrobe.

She hadn't brought anything very chic with her—she only had one really special dress, jade green, smooth-fitting, made in silky Merino wool by one of Australia's top young designers. Deciding to wear that, she hunted out some small gold earrings

and a fine gold chain which matched, a gold link
bracelet watch her stepfather had given her on her
twenty-first birthday. She chose black shoes and
black stockings, some filmy black underwear, laid
them all out on her bed, then went to have a bath.
She wouldn't be nervous of facing the Killanes if she
looked her best.

Prue liked to travel light, with meant jeans and
shorts and thin cotton tops, all uncreasable and easy
to wash. This visit had been intended as a brief one
before she and David headed for France then down
through Spain to the sun again, or maybe to Italy.
They hadn't made any specific plans or booked
anything. David had said, 'Let's free-fall, take it as it
comes!' and she had cheerfully said, 'Yes, let's!' and
each of them had packed the minimum. It would
have been a carefree way of travelling if Prue hadn't
had her father on her mind; she wished now that she
had left this trip to Yorkshire until the end of the
holiday. David wouldn't be in a hospital bed and she
wouldn't be in this bath, dreading the thought of the
dinner party ahead of her!

As time ticked by, she grew more and more edgy,
and her father looked anxiously at her as they drove
to Killane House.

'I'm sure you'll enjoy yourself—they're very
hospitable.'

She dredged up a smile from somewhere. 'I'm fine,
don't worry, Dad.'

He tried to look hopeful, but merely looked
nervous. Five minutes later, they drove up a long,
tree-lined drive and pulled up outside the shabby,
glorious façade of the old house; the car's head-

lights shone over it and Prue gave a gasp as she saw tiny, black shapes stream upwards from under the roof.

'Dad! What on earth . . .?'

James Allardyce laughed. 'Pipistrelle bats—quite harmless!' he said, and just then Josh Killane materialised out of the shadows under the portico. He was in a dinner-jacket and had barely shown up against the unlit stone walls.

'This must be Count Dracula!' Prue muttered, and her father laughed.

'Poor Josh—you have got it in for him! But I must admit he looks the part.'

Josh came down the steps, bent down, nodded to Prue. 'Welcome to our home,' he said formally, opening her door.

She slid out with a shiver of reluctance and he glanced down at her. 'It is quite chilly tonight—come in quickly, it's much warmer in the house now that we've installed central heating. It was a draughty old barn when I was a boy, but it's much more comfortable now.'

'Funny you should compare it to a barn!' said her father. 'Prue just jumped out of her skin when she saw some bats up there.' He pointed upwards. 'Did you know there were bats under the roof, Josh?'

'Yes, of course. They've been there for years, they don't do any harm.' Josh looked mockingly at Prue. 'So you were scared?'

'Of course not,' she said in a crisp voice. 'Just startled.'

Someone else appeared in the doorway; Prue recognised Mrs Killane at once, even though her jet hair was silvered and her slender body had become more rounded with age. Her face seemed quite unlined, her beauty as breathtaking as ever. While Prue stared, James Allardyce moved towards her, and she held out a hand.

'Jim!'

'You look very charming tonight, Lucy,' he murmured in a warm voice, holding her hand while he stared down at her, and Prue felt her own face harden, her mouth become a tight, cold line. They didn't talk to each other like old friends; it was far more than that. She had felt that she would know if they were lovers, and she did. Her mother hadn't been crazy or neurotic; she had been right all along.

'Aren't you coming in?' Josh asked coldly, and she started, giving him a look from under her lashes. He was watching her with enmity; she lifted her lashes and looked back in the same hostile way.

'I suppose so.'

His frown darkened his face. 'What the hell is the matter with you? Are you going to be touchy all evening? Why did you come, if you were in one of your moods?'

'I'm not in one of my moods!' she muttered. 'I don't know what you mean—one of my moods! What moods? You only met me the other day, what do you know about my moods? Anyway, I don't have moods. I'm a very even-tempered person, normally. If I've been touchy when you're around, it's been your fault.'

He laughed furiously. 'Oh, of course, it would be! I've met women like you before. I recognise the attitude. Nothing is ever your fault, is it? Someone else is always to blame—usually some poor bloody man!'

'Don't you swear at me!' said Prue, teeth tight with rage.

'You call that swearing? You've led a sheltered life!'

'And don't sneer,' said Prue.

'For heaven's sake!' he ground out, his face reddening with fury.

'Don't snarl, either,' she said with a peculiar satisfaction in the sight of his temper rising.

He gave a thick, wordless exclamation and grabbed her arm, shaking her. 'Now listen!' he burst out, without saying precisely what she was to listen to!

Prue tried to look as calm as a cucumber. That wasn't how she felt, of course; she was as angry as he was, if for different reasons. Deep inside her she knew that she had deliberately pushed him into this ferocious temper. She wasn't sure why, but she had been possessed of terrible energy and had needed to release it by quarrelling with someone—or, she thought, in a horrified admission just to herself, by making passionate love. Of the two alternatives, given that Josh Killane was the only man around at the moment, quarrelling seemed the wiser choice.

'Get your hands off me!' She glanced past him at the door, in the hope of rescue, but her father and Lucy Killane had vanished.

Josh looked back, too, and Prue took the opportunity to wrench herself free and dart towards the doorway. He caught up with her a few feet from the house, spun her round to face him again.

'Don't you . . .' she began, but he interrupted.

'Will you stop giving me orders? I don't like bossy

women.'

'I don't care what you don't like!' she began, then
his hands closed over her shoulders and lifted her up
until they were face to face. Prue was startled to find
herself looking into his violent, dark eyes, and for a
moment she was too breathless to speak. Josh kissed
her; an angry kiss which forced her lips back on her
teeth and suffocated her. She shut her eyes in shock,
felt his mouth crushed down against hers briefly,
then she was back on the ground, on her own two
feet, but reeling like a drunk.

'And don't tell me! I know!' he said. 'I mustn't kiss
you.'

She didn't have to answer, because while she was
trying to find the words to tell him exactly what she
thought of him, her father appeared in the doorway
and called to them.

'Aren't you two coming in? It's cold out there.'

'Coming,' Prue said in a thin voice, walking
towards him fast, and Josh followed more slowly.
She looked around her as she entered the high-
ceilinged hall; it was unfamiliar. She must have been
here as a child, but she did not recall it. Tonight,
there was a log fire burning in the large stone
fireplace, and great bronze vases of autumn flowers
on either side of the hearth. Lucy Killane stood by a
Georgian table, pouring drinks.

'You remember Mrs Killane, Prue,' James
Allardyce said, introducing them, and Prue held out
her hand politely, with an effort she hoped she hid.

'Of course. Hello, Mrs Killane.'

'It's nice to see you home again, Prue,' Lucy
Killane said, her voice warm as melted honey—but

how real was the sweetness?

'I'm happy to be home.' Prue's glance slid sideways to the other person in the hall, a girl sitting on a red velvet-covered chair, her eyes on her own two hands, which were clasped around her knees. Prue recognised her, too—it was the girl who had been with her father that morning. What had he called her?

'Do you remember my daughter, Lynsey?' asked Lucy Killane, noticing where Prue was looking, and Prue couldn't help giving Josh a quick flick of her angry green eyes. His sister? Not his girlfriend? What had all that been about, then, yesterday morning? What had Lynsey Killane done? He had been so angry and the girl had been so defiant as he'd hustled her away.

'I think so,' Prue said slowly, beginning to remember a much younger girl, skinny and slight with huge eyes. Lynsey Killane had made so little impact that Prue had forgotten about her altogether until now.

'You were much older,' agreed Mrs Killane. 'Lynsey's just eighteen, now.'

'Hello,' Prue said to the other girl, and Lynsey nodded, looking up.

'Hi.' She wasn't exactly unfriendly, but she made it clear that Prue was out of her age group, not someone who could ever become a close friend, which meant that Lynsey couldn't be bothered with her. After giving Prue that cool look, she turned her head to watch the log fire, her long black lashes lying against her cheek, showing Prue her immaculate profile—delicate, half childlike, very lovely.

'What can I get you to drink?' asked Josh, and Prue
accepted a sherry, amber-gold and very sweet.

'Come and sit near the fire,' said Mrs Killane. 'We
like sitting in the hall; it can get too cold in winter, but
at this time of year it is perfect with a big fire, and we
have plenty of logs to burn. Josh thins out the timber
from time to time. We replace each tree with a
sapling, of course; timber is a valuable part of our
income, you have to manage the forestry properly.'
She was talking huskily, sounding a little nervous.

'She isn't interested in estate management,
Mother,' Josh said drily.

'Oh, but I am,' said Prue, not quite honestly, and
wondered yet again at her unvarying impulse to
annoy him. He gave her a look that told her he had
noticed, she needn't think he hadn't, and he didn't
like it—or her—much! She gave him a sweet smile
that told him it was mutual—she didn't like him
much, either!

Nobody else seemed to be aware of their silent
exchange of hostility, although to Prue it was as
obvious as a ten-foot wall.

'What a pity about your fiancé,' said Lucy Killane,
politely changing the subject anyway. 'I hope he isn't
too badly injured?'

'I hope so, too,' Prue said, on a sudden sigh, partly
out of guilt because she was spending more time
hating Josh Killane than she was thinking about
David. 'I should have rung his parents and told
them,' she thought aloud, 'but I wanted to wait until
I knew for certain how he was . . . I don't want them
to drop everything and fly over here if David really
isn't badly hurt, but on the other hand, if it is

serious I know they'd never forgive me if they weren't told. I'm seeing him tomorrow, and I'll ring them afterwards.'

'Where do they live?' Mrs Killane asked.

'Sydney; very near where we lived.' That reminded her of her mother, she frowned and met the other woman's eyes; saw a faint flicker of uneasiness in those dark depths. Lucy Killane was thinking about her mother, too! A telepathic flash passed between them and Lucy Killane paled a little.

Prue went on flatly, 'They were good friends to my mother and me. After she was killed, I don't know what I would have done without them.

'So you've known your fiancé for quite a while,' said Josh, and she nodded. 'A boy and girl affair!' he added drily, making her bristle.

'We're hardly teenagers!'

'He drives like a teenager.'

'That's unfair; just because he had an accident . . .'

'He crashed because he wasn't looking where he was going!'

'How do you know why he crashed?'

'Because I saw him kissing you as he came over the top of that hill!'

Prue felt herself flush hotly. 'He didn't . . .' But she wasn't sure if that was the truth or not; she couldn't actually remember what had been happening in the few moments before the car veered wildly across the road. The shock of the crash had wiped out everything but a vision of Josh Killane's angry, tightened features flashing past them, her own scream of fear, David's shaken exclamation and then the impact as the car hit the stone wall.

'Josh! Stop being so aggressive!' Mrs Killane said anxiously, frowning at her son, whose mouth indented as he shrugged.

'You seem to forget, I could have been put into hospital myself—or killed! And all because this guy hadn't got his mind on the road.'

'Prue is our guest!' his mother warned, looking unhappily at Prue. 'Prue, I'm sorry. Josh has a terrible temper, I'm afraid.'

'I had noticed,' Prue said.

Josh opened his mouth to argue, but James Allardyce beat him to it, hurriedly saying, 'It just occurred to me . . . I'm wall-mending tomorrow morning, Josh, so as Prue needs to be driven to the hospital, maybe I could change my shift with someone else?'

'That won't be easy,' Josh said. 'I had a job fitting that rota together; I don't know who could change shifts with you. Look, I'll drive her to the hospital. I have to drop in there, anyway.'

'I can get a taxi,' Prue hastily said, appalled at the very idea of another confrontation with Josh Killane, but nobody took any notice of her.

'Why do you have to go to the hospital?' Mrs Killane asked Josh.

'I have to call in on old Jack Armsden.'

'Of course, I'd forgotten!' said his mother.

'They had him in there for observation for a week, but he had his operation the day before yesterday, and the ward sister rang me today to say he could have visitors now. I said I'd call in some time tomorrow.'

'Poor old Jack, having a major operation at his age

is no joke,' said James Allardyce.

'Does the hospital think he's going to be OK?' Mrs Killane asked her son, who shrugged, his face wry.

'They weren't saying, but he's a tough old man, I think he has a fair chance of pulling through.'

'He has no family left,' James Allardyce said, looking sombre.

'No,' agreed Josh flatly. 'That's why I must go and see him as soon as possible.'

'Oh, yes, you must!' Mrs Killane agreed. 'Poor man, and he's always so kind. Who's looking after his dogs? I should have thought of that.'

'Don't worry, Mother, I've seen to the dogs, and the canary!'

'Josh thinks of everything!' Lynsey suddenly said in a sniping voice, and her mother frowned at her.

'Yes, he does—whatever is the matter with you, Lynsey? Stop trying to get at your brother all the time!'

'Oh, dear, so sorry,' Lynsey said, getting up and flouncing up the stairs.

'Lynsey! Come back here!' her mother called after her, but got no answer. Flushed and upset, Mrs Killane looked helplessly at Josh.

'What are we going to do with her?'

'She's going back to college soon, that's what we're going to do with her,' he said, frowning in grim irritation.

'Dinner's nearly ready—I'd better go and get her down again!' his mother said, but Josh shook his head.

'Leave her up there. If she's hungry, she'll come down. If she doesn't, she can go without!' He looked at James Allardyce. 'If you get a chance, maybe you could visit Jack Armsden, Jim?'

'Of course I will! Known him all my life, after all.'

'Yes, he's worked on the estate since he was a boy, and his father before him—we're the nearest thing to a family he's got.'

Prue met her father's eyes and James Allardyce explained, 'Jack's wife died years ago—they did have a boy once, when they were young, but he died when he was just a lad, I can't remember what he died of, can you, Lucy?'

'Wasn't it polio? It was very sudden; a tragic business and they could never have another child, she was one of those tiny, frail women. She had tuberculosis—maybe that was what killed the boy, too? I can't quite remember, it was so long ago. Jack was in his early forties, then, and how old is he now?'

'Seventy-two,' said Josh. 'As you say, it was all so long ago. He's been alone for years.'

'Poor old man,' Prue thought aloud, shivering because she remembered how she had felt when her mother was killed and she found herself left alone in the world. She had, at least, had David and his family nearby, to comfort her, though. It must have been much worse for Jack Armsden.

'So as I have to go to the hospital,' Josh repeated, 'I'll take Prue in with me and kill two birds with one stone.'

'Can I come?' Lynsey Killane said from the stairs, making them all jump because they hadn't heard her coming back.

Her brother frowned blackly at her. 'I'm not taking you anywhere!'

'I want to see Jack! I'm fond of him!' She didn't actually stamp her foot, but Prue got the impression she almost did, her lovely face petulant.

'That's a good idea!' Mrs Killane said hurriedly. 'Jack's always been fond of Lynsey, Josh, you know he has . . . why not take her?'

'After the little exhibition she just put on? I didn't hear any apology, either!'

'I'm sorry I lost my temper,' Lynsey said. 'There . . . I've apologised, will you take me tomorrow?'

'I'd love to have company on the drive,' Prue said, and everyone looked at her—Josh furiously, his mother and her father gratefully, Lynsey with the first sign of interest, smiling her little, curling, rather feline smile.

'That's settled, then,' she said.

CHAPTER FOUR

WHEN Prue came down to breakfast next day, her father had already started work, but there was a tall, raw-boned woman in the hall, polishing furniture and leaving a delicious scent of lavender on the air.

She looked round as Prue appeared, nodding. 'Morning. You must be his daughter. He's off out long since.'

Prue detected a note of disapproval in that. Her father had warned her that Betty Cain was blunt and Yorkshire to her fingertips, and this had to be Betty Cain. A woman in her forties, with dark brown hair and a clear, weathered skin, Betty Cain was busy, energetic and not inclined to gossip.

'I've done the kitchen, if you want to get yourself breakfast, but I must get on!' she said, going back to her polishing, and Prue hardly got a word out of her after that.

Josh drove up punctually; Prue got into the back seat, since Lynsey was in the front passenger seat, and they drove most of the way without saying much. When they reached the hospital, they discovered that David was in the same ward as Jack Armsden, although David was in a bed by a window at the end of the room, and the old man was in a bed by the door, where a nurse could keep a constant eye on him. Prue watched Josh and Lynsey stand by the bed; the old man's face was waxy white on the pillow and he had his eyes shut, his lids blue-veined. He looked very old and ill, and she felt a wave of pity for him.

It was a relief to see that David looked better than that! In fact, he waved as she came towards him. Propped up by banked pillows, his head bandaged and his pyjama jacket buttoned over bandages which strapped up his ribs, he looked quite pale, too, but his eyes were cheerful enough.

'Hello, darling! he said, grinning at her.

'I've been so worried about you, but you look great,' she said, bending to kiss him.

'All the better for seeing you, my dear!' he said in a comic wolf's growl, and she laughed, pulling up a chair so that she could sit beside his bed.

'I can see you're feeling better than you did last time I saw you, anyway!'

'You should have seen me yesterday! Strewth, I never thought I'd make it. I'd have made my will if I could have held the pen to sign it.'

'Poor David!' she said, holding his hand and smiling at him. 'I'm very glad you weren't seriously hurt. I was dreading ringing your Mum and Dad if I had to tell them bad news.'

'They know I crashed?' David looked rueful.

'Not yet. I was waiting to find out how badly you were hurt. I didn't want to panic them unnecessarily.'

'Good thinking,' he agreed fervently. 'In fact, don't bother to ring at all. When I'm out of here, I'll send Mum and Dad the odd postcard from Europe, and I'll tell them about the crash when I get back home.'

'David, you can't do that!' Prue was horrified, and he looked sullen.

'Prue, if we tell them they'll make a terrible fuss—you know that!'

She wasn't convinced, her face anxious. 'But when they do find out, they'll be furious.'

'I'll talk them round!' he dismissed, which was typical of David, who was always sure of himself and his ability to twist both his friends and his family round his little finger. 'Now, tell me about your Dad and the farm!'

Prue let him change the subject for the moment, because she didn't want to upset him so soon after the accident. He still looked ill.

She gave him a slightly edited version of her meeting with her father, described the farm in glowing, lyrical terms, and told him how sad she had been to discover that her old dog had died years ago.

'Typical of you to be so upset about it!' he said, smiling at her lovingly.

'You know you would be, in my shoes.' David loved his own dog back at home in Sydney. 'You'd go spare if you got home and found that Dodger had died while you were away!'

'True,' he admitted ruefully. 'He's a stupid old fool, but dogs do get to you, don't they? Cats I can take or leave, but I would miss old Dodger.'

'And your mother would cry her eyes out,' Prue said. 'Although I think she loves Dodger because he's your dog.' She gave him a coaxing, smiling look. 'David, I really think I ought to ring her! She might be hurt if we didn't tell them about the accident until weeks later. They would feel shut out, excluded.'

'They'll forgive me!' he said with utter conviction, and she sighed uneasily.

'I'm not so sure they'll forgive me!' His mother would certainly think that she should have got in touch with them; she would blame Prue, not her own son, and she would be quite right. 'I ought to tell them, David! They have a right to know.'

His mouth turned down and his face took on that sulky look again.

'Don't nag me, Prue!'

'I'm not nagging, I just think . . .'

'They're my parents, not yours, for heaven's sake!' She bit her lip. 'I know, but . . .'

'I'm a big boy now, I don't want them rushing over here. Mum will cry over me, and Dad's going to blame me for the crash. He's always saying I'm a rotten driver, you know that. He never trusts me with his bloody car. When he hears there was a crash, he'll think it was my fault, sure as hell. If they fly over here, they'll want me to go home right away, but I've come a long way round the world to see Europe and, accident or no accident, I'm not going home until I've seen it.'

'But, David . . .' she began, and he interrupted her, his voice very loud.

'Will you stop whingeing? Just do what I say, OK?'

He was flushed, his eyes too bright. Prue stared at him, suddenly seeing that he really wasn't very well yet; he was behaving like a petulant little brat, and that wasn't like David at all! She should be humouring him—not arguing with him and upsetting him all the time.

Their quarrel had attracted the attention of the nurse in charge of the ward. She came over to the bed, eyed David with a professional blankness, then looked reprovingly at Prue.

'I think perhaps you had better go now. Mr Henley is still under sedation, and he really ought to get some more rest.'

'I'm not that crook, Nurse!' David said, at once resisting any suggestion that he might be ill.

'I don't think you're the best judge of that, Mr Henley!' the nurse merely said, her lips thinning.

David made a face at Prue, who got up, under the nurse's disapproving eyes; feeling gawky and sheepish, as she usually had when she was a teenager, all long legs and untidy red hair, confronted by hostile, critical adults.

David's mouth had a weary droop. Prue bent to kiss it, but he turned his head away at the last moment, and she kissed his cheek, knowing he had moved deliberately, he was still cross with her.

'I'm sorry,' she whispered, close to his ear. 'I won't ring your parents, don't be cross, darling. Love you.'

The waiting nurse coughed meaningfully; one neat black shoe tapping as she consulted the watch pinned to her apron.

'Come tomorrow,' David said, relenting enough to smile, so Prue turned and walked away down the ward. She paused at the swing doors to blow him a kiss, but he was leaning back against his pillows, his eyes closed, the flush still high on his cheeks. Feeling very guilty, Prue walked back through the hospital to the car park, to wait for Josh Killane and his sister, whom she had noticed still sitting beside the old man's bed. Prue hadn't actually looked in their direction, she had merely observed them out of the corner of her eye. They didn't seem to be talking; she didn't hear voices from the bed and the old man appeared to be sleeping, so she imagined it would not be long before they joined her.

The car was locked, so she walked around the gardens adjoining the car park. Autumn winds had strewn the wet grass with leaves; bronze, russet, and gold, a few spectral, like grey lace stretched over a fan of fine bones, all colour bleached out of them by the rain. Prue walked through them, enjoying their rustle, kicking them up and watching them fly.

She was thinking about David as she walked, worried by his unusual mood. The accident had been a bad shock; he had lost blood, a lot of it, he had had an operation, he had broken ribs and a head injury—she should have realised how much all that would have affected him, but she had been stupid. She had been insensitive with him, and she could kick herself. Why on earth did you argue with him? she asked herself fiercely.

She shouldn't have been surprised by David's reaction to the idea of his parents being told about the accident. He loved his parents, of course, and she knew how much they loved him. When they heard the news, they would have flown over here, and they would have wanted David to go back to Australia with them.

He was right about something else! His father would undoubtedly have guessed that the accident was David's fault. He would be right, too, wouldn't he? David had been driving carelessly; it was pure luck that neither of them had been killed. Well, luck and the quick-wittedness of Josh Killane. He could so easily have smashed straight into their car, but he had veered away without crashing. David hadn't reacted fast enough; he had driven their car into that wall.

This wasn't the first accident he had had, either, as his father would have reminded him. He had scraped a wing here, dented a bumper there, but none of his other accidents had been serious or even very expensive on the garage bills. All the same, his father would have a few things to say about this crash—and David hated being criticised or blamed. He was a sunny character, but only so long as things went well; he liked to skate over life's surface, having fun and enjoying himself, laid-back and casual, a little lazy, and reluctant to accept responsibility even for himself. He wanted to live in the sun—he ran from bad weather.

David's idea of a marvellous life was to laze on the beach all day; a little swim or a ride on the surf, then a little barbecue with their mates, some partying and a few tubes of Fosters and maybe sleep in a hammock on the terrace in the warm night air. Prue had always thought it sounded a good life, too.

She and David had had the odd argument in the past but, like his other accidents, their arguments had never been serious or meant anything, and she wished she hadn't argued with him today. He wasn't himself, she should have left the subject until he was really better.

The grate of feet on gravel made her turn her head.

Josh was walking towards her, dark hair windblown, lean body moving gracefully in the old tweed jacket and grey flannel trousers. He was alone, and she looked past him towards the car, but there was no sign of Lynsey in it.

'That was a short visit,' he said drily, and she flushed, at once ready to take umbrage.

'David isn't very well yet—the ward sister thought I shouldn't stay long.'

'Why are you so defensive?'

'I'm not!' She wasn't defensive, she was irritated. He was commenting on her private life again. Why couldn't he mind his own business? 'Where's your sister?' she asked, to change the subject rather than because she cared.

'Visiting your fiancé,' he drawled, and Prue stared at him. 'She noticed you hadn't brought him any flowers, so she went to the hospital shop and bought him some.'

He seemed to find it amusing; Prue didn't. 'How thoughtful of her,' she said through her teeth. His sister had some of his interfering tendencies, did she? Prue hadn't forgotten to buy David flowers; it simply hadn't occurred to her to take him any. Back home he would have felt a fool if she was seen giving him a bunch of flowers. His mates would have teased him about it. Prue wondered what he had said when an unknown girl came up to him, gave him a bouquet and chatted him up.

Of course, Lynsey was very young and beautiful. David would have been flattered by her attention; it might have put him back into his usual cheerful, easy-going temper.

'You resent it,' Josh thought aloud, watching her.

'No, I'm grateful to her,' Prue said.

'Hmm,' he said, unconvinced, then eyed her thoughtfully. 'I rather got the idea you were having a row with him. Anything wrong?'

He was too observant, thought Prue, fighting to look blank. 'Nothing is wrong,' she insisted.

'Hmm,' he said again, maddeningly.

Lynsey came sauntering out of the hospital entrance just then. She joined them, tilting her chin defiantly at Prue.

'I told her you had taken her fiancé some flowers,' Josh said.

'I hope you didn't mind,' Lynsey said in an offhand voice which clearly conveyed that she didn't care whether Prue minded or not.

'It was very kind of you, thank you,' said Prue. 'He isn't too well yet, and I'm sure your flowers cheered him up.'

'He seemed to like them,' Lynsey said, sliding her slender body into the back seat of the car, and managing to imply that Prue should have thought of taking David flowers, which so annoyed Prue that before she knew what was happening she found herself in the front seat next to Josh.

As they drove off, Lynsey leaned forward and said to her brother, 'Drop me off at the village, will you? I want to call in on an old pal.'

'Who?' he asked, driving steadily, his eyes on the road.

'Don't be nosy, Josh!' Lynsey snapped.

Prue eyed him blandly out of the corner of her eye; Josh sensed as much and turned his head to look at her, his mouth hard.

'Why can't you say who you're meeting?' he still insisted to Lynsey.

'Oh, Caroline, if you absolutely must know!'

'Why all the secrecy about meeting Caroline?' he demanded, and Prue watched Lynsey in the wing mirror, wondering if it was really this Caroline she was meeting, or if she had rapidly invented that story to placate her brother?

'Why do I always have to tell you everything I'm doing?' Lynsey muttered.

He made an impatient face. 'Oh, well! Don't be late back, then!'

'Nag, nag, nag.'

'You know Mother will start worrying if you're out for hours, and we don't know where you are!'

A heavy sigh was all the answer he got, and he drove in silence for ten minutes. When they entered the village at the heart of the valley, Lynsey said quickly, 'Drop me at the post office, would you? I promised David I'd buy him a postcard of the village.'

Prue gave her a startled look. David? Lynsey used his name pretty casually, considering they had only met for the first time today, and just for five minutes too! Had he really asked Lynsey to buy him a postcard? Or had she offered to? Lynsey ignored her, seemingly unaware of her frowning scrutiny.

Josh stopped the car and Lynsey got out, slamming the door behind her. As they drove on, Prue glanced back and saw Lynsey going into the post office. The Killanes were an interfering family! What did Lynsey think she was doing, chatting David up, taking him flowers, buying things for him? Prue felt guilty because she should have thought of asking David if he needed anything instead of quarrelling with him over his parents, and guilt made her angry with Lynsey for having the cheek to do what Prue should have done.

'Is your sister in training to be a social worker?' she asked Josh coldly.

'Miaow,' he said, grinning, but she decided to ignore that.

'When exactly does she go back to her college?'

'Oh, soon, don't worry.' He seemed to find all this very amusing; Prue didn't.

'I am not worrying,' she said with dignity, and he laughed, which somewhat spoiled the effect.

'Oh, no?'

'No!' she insisted.

'Sure you aren't jealous because she's taking an interest in your fiancé?'

'She's just a kid,' Prue dismissed. 'Does she often get crushes on people? I know some teenagers do.'

'Would you call her a teenager?'

'She's eighteen, what else could you call her?'

He turned in through the gates of the farm, considering that question. 'Well, I'd have said Lynsey was a young woman—she's legally of age and could get married, drive a car or fight for her country, so I don't think I'd call her a teenager.' He pulled up outside the house and turned in his seat to face Prue, his face quizzical. 'Take no notice of her. She's romantic by nature. Your fiancé's not bad-looking, he's lying helpless in a hospital bed and he's far away from his home and family—that makes him irresistible to a girl like my sister!'

Prue listened and watched him, her view of him breaking up and reforming in a dizzying fashion. Sometimes she wished she had a gun to shoot him with, yet sometimes, as now, he was gentle and thoughtful and kind. The Killanes were a puzzling family; an enigma.

He gave her a crooked little smile, one eyebrow slanting upwards. 'What's on your mind now?'

'Sorry?' She started, looking into his jet-black eyes and seeing little golden flecks around the pupil which she had never noticed before—had they been there? or was it the reflection of the autumn sun she was seeing?

'You were staring at me in an odd way,' he said softly, looking deep into her green eyes, his face very close.

'I was thinking,' she said in some confusion, feeling hot colour wash upwards to her hairline.

'Your eyes are the brightest green I've ever seen,' he murmured, a hand lazily reaching out to touch her flushed cheek.

She jumped back from that contact, looking away. 'Thanks for the lift, I'd better find my father,' she muttered, grabbing for the door handle and opening the car.

Josh didn't argue; he swung round in his own seat and got out, too, facing her across the top of the car. 'You won't find him in the house. He'll have left the key under a flowerpot on the kitchen window-sill, though, so you can get in easily enough. I'll show you.'

'Where has Dad gone?' she asked, frowning as she

hurried to keep up with his stride.

'He's up on Windacre Hill, mending walls.'

'Oh, of course, I'd forgotten! Stupid of me, I don't know how I came to forget that.'

Josh gave her a wry look. 'Something else on your mind?' The softly murmured words had an insinuating quality which made Prue uneasy. They reached the back of the house, and Josh picked up a flowerpot on the window-sill and retrieved the key lying there.

'Thank you,' Prue said stiffly, reaching for it, but he was already at the back door, fitting the key into the lock. 'I can manage now,' she insisted, but he took no notice, pushing the door open and waving her into the house. She didn't quite like to slam the door in his face, so he followed her inside, closing the outer door behind him, and Prue's nerves leapt violently.

'Well, thank you,' she said, not wishing to be rude to him when he had taken so much trouble to be helpful, yet rather edgy about being alone with him again in the empty house. Whenever they were alone together, she felt this strange sensation: a mixture of heat and rage she didn't understand. She could not reason herself out of it; the chemical reaction was explosive, she felt it happening inside her now, an energy which built up until the pressure of it had terrible force. She had never known anything like it before and it disturbed her.

'He won't be back until it's dark,' Josh said coolly, totally unaware of what she felt, thank heavens.

'That's OK, it doesn't matter, I'll be all right,' she muttered, avoiding his much too observant eyes.

'Why not come home with me and have tea with my mother?'

She shook her head. 'Thank you, but . . .'

'She'd be very glad to see you!'

'I really must do some washing and ironing,' Prue said, a chilliness creeping into her voice at the very mention of Mrs Killane.

He watched her, a black frown drawing his brows together. 'What have you got against my mother?'

The attack was abrupt and unexpected, and her eyes lifted, wide and startled.

'Wh-why . . . what makes you think I . . .'

'Your face changes every time she's mentioned. Do you think you can hide dislike? You can't, you know—not if it's strong enough, and you really don't like my mother, do you?'

Prue was as pale now as she had been flushed. 'No, I don't—and I'm sure you know why!' she snapped.

'You tell me,' he said quietly, the lines of his face taut and angular.

'Don't pretend you don't know all about it! You're not stupid, and if a stranger like me can see it so clearly, then you must have noticed it years ago!'

'What are we talking about? What can you see so clearly?'

She took a fierce breath, trembling with anger. 'Your mother—and my father!'

'Ah,' he said, his eyes black ice.

'I know about them! My mother told me the whole story, and when I saw them together, after I got here, I knew she had told me the truth, and you must know all about it, too. You couldn't be that blind!'

He stood there, looming above her, staring down in

piercing scrutiny as if he looked right through her eyes into her very mind, and did not like what he saw. He might know the truth about his mother's long love-affair with James Allardyce, but he did not like to have it talked about. He preferred to shut his eyes to it, no doubt, as his father must have done for years. But perhaps his father hadn't known? As a child, she had often seen the Killanes together, and there had been a warm, affectionate feeling between them, which had particularly struck her because it was so different from the way things were between her own parents.

She had been too young then to know anything of the more intimate side of love; she wouldn't have recognised physical attraction if she had seen it, she had no idea what sort of love there had been between Josh's parents, but she did know one thing—they had cared for each other, they had been happy together, so perhaps Henry Killane had never guessed what was going on between his wife and James Allardyce?

Josh suddenly swung round and picked up the kettle, filling it from the tap.

'What are you doing?' Prue asked, taken aback.

'Making some tea.' He put the kettle on the stove without looking at her, and she scowled at him.

'I'd rather you left now, please!'

'I have a few things I want to say to you, first,' he bit out. 'And I need a cup of strong tea before I say them.' He found big, yellow, earthenware mugs hanging on a line of hooks, opened the fridge and found milk, dug out some teaspoons, while Prue watched him, seething.

'I like the way you make yourself at home in my

father's house!'

Josh ignored her, spooning tea into the teapot.

'I suppose just because your family own the land you think you own all the people who work on it, too!' she threw angrily at him.

He spun round, then, blazing with fury; she got the feeling he was going to hit her and stumbled backwards, which made him bare his teeth in a mimicry of a smile.

'Yes, I ought to slap you! You can think yourself lucky I have more self-control than you do, or I would! Now, just shut up while I finish making this tea.'

'Don't you shout at me!' Her brief flash of fear over, Prue was in a belligerent mood again, but so was Josh.

'Sit down!' he bellowed, and something about the way he looked at her made Prue obey. He made the tea and stirred the pot, then she watched him pour the tea. What did he have to say to her? she wondered, scowling. Or could she guess!

'I suppose you'd like me to pretend not to know about their affair?' she broke out as he turned, a mug in each hand. 'Well, don't worry, I won't say anything—I haven't mentioned it to my father and I wouldn't have said anything to you if you hadn't made me!'

'You don't have to say anything! You have other ways of getting your point across!' He handed her a mug in a very ungracious fashion, shoving it into her hands so that she almost dropped it. 'I don't like the way you watch my mother, or the look in your eyes every time you see her look at your father.'

'Sorry!' she snapped. 'I have my reasons—but I don't expect you to understand! It wasn't you and your mother who were driven away from home—it was me and mine! If I'm bitter, it's because I had to live with an embittered woman for years. All she talked about was what your mother had done to her. God forgive me, at times I was so sick of listening that I started blaming her! I thought she was a neurotic who'd invented it all. But she hadn't made it up, had she? It was all true.'

Josh leaned on the wall, facing her, nursing his mug between both hands, his angry, dark eyes fixed on her.

'Is that why you came back?' he asked slowly. 'Not to see your father again—but to find out how much truth there was in your mother's stories?'

Prue shrugged. 'I came for lots of reasons! I wanted to see my father again, and I wanted to see Yorkshire and the farm and the village, and everything I remembered, but I wanted to find out the truth, too.'

'Sure you didn't want to cause the maximum amount of damage to everyone who'd hurt your mother?' Josh asked in a neutral voice, and she shook her head, her face resentful.

'I don't think like that! You may be cold-blooded enough to go looking for revenge, but I'm not.'

'Oh, I wouldn't dream of suggesting you're cold-blooded,' he said drily, and smiled in a way that made Prue uneasy. She was afraid of saying the wrong thing, so she silently gave him a hostile stare. After waiting a moment, Josh added softly, 'Although after watching you with your fiancé today, I did wonder!'

That hit her where she was vulnerable! Ever since she left the hospital, she had been feeling guilty over quarrelling with David while he was ill. She blazed up, glaring at Josh. 'What do you mean by that?'

'Do you sleep with him?' he enquired in an apparently casual voice, and she turned scarlet, because he had unerringly touched on another painful question. David had wanted to make love to her months ago, but, perhaps because of the disaster love had been to her parents, she hadn't felt she could yet give herself, she wasn't ready for that final commitment and, although he had sighed, David had said he understood.

Josh's eyes glittered with a disturbing triumph as he watched her betraying expression. 'So you don't! I suspected as much.'

'Mind your own business!' she snarled, hating him—how on earth had he guessed?

'Does he know?' Josh drawled, perplexing her.

'Know?' she stammered, bewildered by the question.

'That your mother locked you up in deep freeze years ago and you don't know the first thing about loving anyone?'

She threw the tea at him on impulse; she hadn't intended to do it, she just hurled the mug, and Josh Killane must have had good reflexes because he ducked before the scalding hot tea reached him. He didn't escape entirely, though; Prue's aim was better than she had ever suspected. Swearing furiously, Josh looked down at his shirt and jacket—both tea-stained.

Prue wasn't surprised by the language, she had

heard worse. She was afraid of Josh in a temper, though. He was frightening when he looked like that, and she was alarmed enough to wish she hadn't done it.

'You crazy little bitch!' he called her, reaching for her with violent hands, and she fled, hearing him right behind her, and catching up fast. She slammed the kitchen door behind her and managed to get to the stairs before he got the door open again, which gave her a slight lead in their race, but he still caught up with her on the landing. By then, Prue was in a feverish state; half fear, half guilt.

She should have apologised, but as his powerful hands grabbed her she panicked and hit him, and this time she did connect with his face. The dramatic sound of the slap was probably worse that the actual impact, but both of them were taken aback.

Josh swore some more, the livid mark of her fingers standing out on his darkly flushed skin. His hands fastened on her wrists, yanked her arms down by her sides, and slammed her up against the wall. He held her there with his body; she felt the lean weight, the muscles backing up his insistence. The breath was almost knocked out of her; she had to fight for breath before she could get a word out.

'Get your damned hands off me!' she raged, and Josh raged back.

'You don't chuck a mug of hot tea over me and get away scot-free, so don't think it!'

Prue swallowed, her head swimming and a sick tension cramping her stomach. She couldn't free herself and she couldn't stand the enforced contact; the last thing she wanted was a sensual awareness of him, but how could she be unaware of his body when it touched hers so intimately? She might ignore what he said; she could never ignore what he was doing. When he breathed she felt it; she almost heard the beating of his heart; his face was inches away, his thigh pushed against her own.

'All right,' she muttered, eyes restlessly evading the pressure of his angry stare, 'I'm sorry! There, will that do? Let me go!'

'Is that supposed to be an apology? Why the hell did you throw that tea over me, anyway?'

'I lost my temper!'

'Oh, it's OK to throw things at someone when you've lost your temper, is it?' he sarcastically drawled, black-browed.

'You insulted me,' she said, feeling childish.

'I told you the truth; it was time you faced it.'

'It wasn't the truth!'

'Oh, yes, it was! Your mother was a neurotic and she screwed you up, too. You're more worked up over what happened years ago to someone else than you are over this guy you're supposed to love!'

'Don't be ridiculous, I . . .'

'You ignored your father after your mother took you to Australia! You didn't answer his letters, although you must have known from them that he loved and missed you, and you didn't come here now because you wanted to tell him you were sorry, or to get to know him again. Why did you come? I wonder if you didn't have doubts about your mother, at last. Did you come to find out whether she was a much wronged woman—or a hysterical neurotic?'

'In some ways, maybe she was!' Prue muttered, hating him. 'But that doesn't mean she wasn't right about your mother and my father. I don't suppose you like admitting it, but they're lovers and have been for years. That's what pushed my mother over the edge. Something made her the way she was!'

'And in her turn, she made you the way you are!' Josh said, and she looked up at him angrily, then froze as she realised how close his face was, so close that she could read every fine line, every pore in his skin, the shadows along his jaw where he needed to shave, the firm moulding of his mouth, the veining on his lids, the black brows and eyelashes.

'I love David!' she said unsteadily, as though by mentioning David's name she could erect a wall between herself and Josh.

His mouth silenced the words; she saw it coming down towards her and she could have turned away, but a terrifyingly intense need consumed her. It wasn't desire or passion, it was an elemental drive like the force that feeds the wind or the tide. She met his mouth angrily, and they kissed like enemies; fighting, not making love, again and again, their bodies clamped together in mortal combat. He was no longer holding her wrists, and she could have got away if she had tried. She didn't try; she had hold of him, her hands attacking him, her nails sinking into his throat, clutching his hair, gripping his shoulders, her eyes shut and her body shaking, until the burning heat went out of her and she pulled her head back.

'No!' she said in a thick voice, feeling sick. 'Go away! Just go away, for God's sake!'

Josh let go of her without argument, and before he

could say anything Prue dived past him and ran into her bedroom, slamming the door and locking it. She leaned there, trembling, hating herself. She loved David, she had loved him for years; she couldn't wait to marry him. There had never been an instant's doubt about how she felt, and there wasn't now. What in heaven's name was wrong with her? She hated Josh Killane as much as she loved David—why, oh, why, had she let him make love to her?

It had happened too suddenly, and yet at the same time, if she was honest, she knew it hadn't been any surprise. She had felt it coming ever since they first met. She couldn't put a name to it, but it had been threatening her on the shadowy outskirts of her consciousness, like a coming hurricane you couldn't see or feel yet, but which all your instincts told you was coming. She shouldn't have let it take her over, though, she should have fought it; why hadn't she fought it?

Cold tears dripped through her closed lids; she tasted their salt on her lips and her whole body seemed cold, too. She felt she would never be warm or happy again. Depression centred on her like a dark cloud. She saw David's face inside her head; she had never had any other boyfriend. David was her first and only one; she had always been totally faithful . . . until now!

What would David think if he ever found out? Hot waves of shame swept over her at the very idea of him knowing. He would be so hurt. What could she ever say to him, how on earth could she explain something so tawdry and unforgivable?

Of course, there were excuses . . . she came up with

them grimly, knowing none of them excused anything. She was lonely, she missed David, she was on edge because she was back home for the first time in years, she was still upset over her mother's death, she was disturbed because of the affair between her father and Josh's mother.

Oh, yes, there were excuses—but she dismissed them all as feeble. She was disgusted with herself for acting like some sex-starved adolescent, especially as she didn't even like the man!

She heard the sound of Josh's car driving away, and with a sigh of relief she walked rather unsteadily to the window to watch him vanish down the drive. At least he had gone, she could relax, try to make her way back to some pretence of normality before her father got home. She went into the bathroom, stripped, showered in almost cold water, obsessively scrubbing her body from her hair down to her feet, and towelling herself angrily. She had needed to cleanse herself of the heat, the sweat, left after those moments in Josh's arms. She would never rid herself of the shame of feeling that way.

She put on clean clothes: an immaculate, tailored white shirt, a chunky black woollen cardigan, a pair of black denims belted tightly at the waist—an outfit which made her look capable rather than sexy and gave her a safer feeling. After she had blowdried her hair, she gathered up all the clothes she had taken off and went downstairs to put them straight into the washing machine in the utility room leading off the kitchen. She didn't stop to ask herself why she felt she must wash them at once; she didn't ask herself why she had deliberately not put on any more make-up or why she was dressed with such neutral neatness. She just threw her clothes into the washing machine and started the process, then went into the kitchen and emptied the teapot, washed it up, washed up the cups, the spoons, the milk jug—everything Josh had touched or used. Her movements had an obsessive intensity; she was pale and her features were rigid.

She made herself a cup of instant coffee in a new cup, and then she sat down and listened to the silence all around her, feeling very alone, and wishing her father would come home.

Josh Killane shouldn't have said she didn't care about her father; it wasn't true, he didn't understand. How could she explain to anyone the complexities of betrayal and loyalty the split between her parents had set up in her mind? If she loved her father, she was disloyal to her mother—if she betrayed her mother, she hurt herself as well as him.

She had come back here to find out how she felt, to resolve a painful situation, uncover the reality of a nightmare she had lived with for years . . . but had she only made things worse by coming back? Should she have stayed away for ever?

CHAPTER FIVE

HER father drove her to see David next day, and Prue was relieved to find him looking much better. He was looking more cheerful, too, and when she stammered out an apology for their quarrel the previous day, he shook his head at her, making a wry face.

'No! It was as much my fault as yours. I was feeling so rotten, it made me touchy. I think it's these damn pills they've got me on; you should see them, big as horse pills and twice as nasty, and you know how I hate taking any sort of medicine. I hate being ill, come to that! I feel damn stupid stuck in this bed when I should be having a great time with you, and most of all, I hate having to yell for a nurse every time I want to go to the toilet.'

'Oh, poor darling,' she said, chuckling. David was himself again and she felt a great wave of warmth towards him, a loving tenderness which was nothing like the terrifying intensity she had felt yesterday in Josh Killane's arms. That had left her appalled and sick. She couldn't even contemplate what it would be like to live with such emotions, but she knew one thing for certain—she would always be contented living with David.

'You were right, anyway!' he said. 'That's partly why I was so mad! You were only telling me what I was secretly thinking, myself. I knew Mum and Dad would kick up merry hell if I didn't let them know I'd been in an accident. I just couldn't face the thought of them rushing over here.'

'I'll ring them right away, and do my best to reassure them!' Prue said, relieved, and David smiled at her.

'No need. I rang them myself an hour ago. Well, I rang Mum—Dad wasn't around.'

'What did she say?' Prue began to feel guilty again; she should have rung the Henleys, she owed it to them, and they would quite rightly blame her for not letting them know about the accident at once!

'I played it down a bit,' David said, grinning wickedly at her.

'What does that mean?' she asked, frowning with concern.

'Oh, I said I'd come off lightly—a couple of broken ribs and a bump on the head, that was all. I didn't tell them about the operation or that one of my ribs had pierced my left lung.'

'What?' Prue went white. 'A rib . . . pierced your lung?' She stared in stunned dismay. 'I had no idea your operation was that serious! They didn't tell me anything was wrong with your lung!'

'They didn't?' he said without surprise, making her wonder if he had asked the hospital authorities not to tell her. 'Sneaky lot, aren't they?' But then he went on, 'They didn't even tell me until this morning.'

Prue studied him anxiously. The injury sounded horrific, but David seemed to be breathing OK and he had quite a good colour now, compared with the way he had looked yesterday.

She determined to seize the first opportunity which came her way to talk to the surgeon who had performed the operation. Why hadn't they told her about this? Why keep it a secret? But then, she hadn't asked them exactly what sort of operation they had performed—she had been in a state of shock herself, of course.

'But how on earth did it happen?' she asked.

'They said I'd got typical steering-wheel injuries,' David said cheerfully. 'When we crashed, I was sort of impacted into the wheel.'

She winced. 'Don't!'

David wasn't listening; he was too fascinated by the details of his accident. 'In fact, I was lucky we didn't hit the wall harder, or I might have crushed my ribcage altogether. As it was, I came off lightly.'

'Lightly?' she grimaced, her eyes ruefully admiring. It was typical of David to shrug off his accident. He wouldn't even take that seriously. She smiled at him, then asked with anxiety, 'What did your mother say? Didn't she ask why I hadn't rung?'

'She asked if you were badly hurt, were you in hospital . . .' David grinned. 'You know my Ma. I told her you'd been in hospital too, but they'd just discharged you. I said you'd be calling her later, but I'd wanted to talk to her myself first.'

She smiled at him. 'You're so tactful!' He had pleased his mother by saying that, and made sure that Mrs Henley wouldn't be angry with Prue for not ringing earlier.

'I know, I'm a marvel,' he said modestly, winking.

'She did start off by saying they ought to come over, but I said I'd be out of here any day and we'd be on our way to Paris.'

'And she didn't argue?' Prue was amazed, knowing his mother.

'She tried to,' David admitted, eyes amused. 'But I told her she was a silly old chuck and I was fine. So when you talk to her, don't tell it any other way, OK?'

'OK,' she said, because he did look miles better than he had the day before, and she was feeling guilty about David, she wanted to please him. 'Anything I can get you, darling?' she asked, looking at the flowers on his bedside locker. Those must be the ones Lynsey Killane had brought him; they were hothouse carnations, pink and cream and white. At this time of year, no doubt very expensive.

David saw her looking at them and grinned. 'Hey, some gorgeous-looking bird brought those in! She said she knew you, your father's a neighbour, or something? Is that right?'

Prue nodded. 'Lynsey Killane.'

'That's her!'

'Her family owns my father's farm,' she said, and David stared blankly.

'Owns it? I thought he . . .'

'No, he isn't the owner, he's the tenant. The Killanes have several farms; they run the biggest, and have tenants on the others. My family have been their tenants for several generations.'

'So your father can't leave the farm to you?' David asked, looking at her with sympathy.

'No, the farm will go back to the Killane estate!

Maybe if I had been a son, they might have let me take over from my father, but as it is . . .' She shrugged.

'Pretty feudal stuff, isn't it?' David said and she nodded wryly.

'I couldn't put it better myself! Feudal is the word.' It fitted more than the situation, come to that—it described Josh Killane perfectly! From the minute she'd met him, Prue had resented his manner; he was overbearing and dictatorial—and loved to act the part of a feudal overlord. Nobody seemed to have told him what century this was!

'It must bug you,' said David, and she started.

'What must?'

'Knowing that your father can't leave you the farm!' he said, surprised by her bewilderment.

'I wouldn't want it, anyway,' Prue said. 'I'm no farmer—but I suppose it isn't very fair after all the years Dad has spent farming the land.' She wasn't too agitated about the injustice, however, because she had never wanted the farm or thought at all about what her father might or might not leave her in his will.

'I've often thought I'd like to have a shot at farming!' David said casually, and she gave him a surprised look.

'Really? You never said so before.'

'Haven't I?' He grinned, eyes teasing. 'Well, it is just one of my many ambitions, of course! I'd like to be an astronaut, too! Do you think it's too late to start the training?'

'Yes,' Prue said, laughing at him because he was playing the fool. David often did that; he was lighthearted, you shouldn't take him too seriously because he didn't take himself seriously. She had never heard him admit to having any ambitions at all; he wanted to enjoy life, not work at it, and most ambitions necessitated quite a bit of work if you were ever to get anywhere.

'Are the Killanes a big family?' he asked, and she shook her head.

'Lynsey has a brother, Josh—he was the driver we nearly collided with!'

'Yes, so his sister said. I can't actually remember him, the accident is a bit of a blur to me. Does he bear me any grudge? She said he wasn't hurt, but I guess he must have been shaken up.'

'He was a little scathing,' she said shortly.

David eyed her, raising an eyebrow. 'You don't like him?'

She shrugged, watching David take a sip of water from his glass.

'What sort of fella is he?' he asked, putting the glass back on his bedside table.

'Formidable,' she said drily. 'A tough character, but then he is a Killane, and they're all very sure of themselves.'

'I suppose you knew him when you lived here as a child?'

'I barely remember him, I was too young to have much to do with the Killanes in those days. He seems to have a finger in most pies around here. Even in the hospital, I've noticed, everyone treats him like God, or at least one of God's executives!'

David laughed, then winced as though laughing made his ribs hurt, and Prue gave him a worried look. Maybe she should leave soon? He was probably getting tired. Prue glanced at the clock. The time had flown.

'You know, I can see your hackles from here!' said David, watching her. 'Did he try to push you around, this divine executive?' He was amused, but Prue didn't smile back this time. She wished he would stop talking about Josh.

'He tried!' she said through her teeth.

She couldn't tell David how she felt about Josh Killane, and that gave her a jab of mingled rage and pain because she was deceiving David, something she had never done before! In the past, she would have told David at once if another man made a pass at her, but for some reason she just couldn't bring herself to tell him about Josh. Was she afraid of what David might do . . . or afraid of what she herself might betray? David knew her so well!

'But failed?' David grinned teasingly at her. When they were just kids, he had got a lot of fun out of watching her fight anyone who tried to bully her; and not much had changed over the years. Prue was still the one who flared up and fought back; David was the lazy, casual, easy-going one, who took life as it came and seemed to laugh at things that made her furious.

She shrugged. 'Let's just say I don't much care for Mr Josh Killane!'

The bell signalling the end of visiting hour began to ring as she was speaking, and Prue jumped up and made a hurried farewell, relieved that the conversation had been interrupted there.

'I'll see you tomorrow—I'm sorry I can't come back

again today, but I don't really like to ask my father to drive me here twice a day, and the hire car is still being repaired.'

David grimaced. 'Good grief, I hadn't thought of garage bills! Tell me the worst—how much is it going to cost?'

'Don't worry. The insurance will pay, that's all dealt with,' she said, kissing him goodbye.

That was something else she didn't want to tell him about! Josh had dealt with their car while Prue was in hospital, and when she'd questioned him, Josh had told her not to bother about it, he had seen to all the financial arrangements. Prue had some idea that the hire car company insurance covered the accident, but tomorrow she would insist on finding out the exact position. For the moment, she did not want David getting agitated over it. He might well ask why Josh had taken charge like that. Of course, it was utterly typical of Josh to be thoughtful and efficient, even in the tiniest details; and she ought to be grateful to him for saving her all that trouble, but she found herself resenting that, too, because it was so typical. He took too much on himself!

What had David said . . . feudal? Yes, the word fitted Josh perfectly; he was a feudal overlord from his black Norman head to his black boots.

'Anything I can get you?' she asked David almost pleadingly, out of her feelings of guilt and contrition.

'Sports magazines, anything light to read—a good thriller, maybe!' he said. 'No more fruit, darling! No food of any kind!' She had brought him fruit, chocolate, even some speckled brown free-range eggs from the farm, laid by one of her father's pretty little Bantam hens that morning!

'I'll never be able to eat my way through this lot as it is!' David said, eyeing the collection assembled on top of his locker.

She found her father in his car in the hospital car park. 'How was he? When am I going to meet him?' he asked as they drove off.

'He's much better, and why not come and meet him tomorrow?' she said, smiling. 'You'll like him.'

He did, of course, immediately. David was easy to like, he made friends without even trying, with that lazy, friendly grin of his; and, in his turn, David was determined to like her father, so of course, he did. There was goodwill on both sides and each of them was delighted to find it so easy to like the other.

'When they let you leave hospital, you must come and stay for a while,' her father told him. 'I'll do my best to see you don't get bored. I suppose a sheep farm isn't the most exciting place in the world, but . . .'

'I've often thought I'd like to farm,' David said, as he had said to Prue, and she gave him a laughing glance, still amused by the idea.

It was the right thing to say to her father, though. He was quite delighted and happily told David all about the farm.

Prue hadn't seen Josh for several days now; she was rather relieved and hoped he would stay away altogether until she and David had left Yorkshire. But, of course, Josh had to work closely with her father, as with all the other tenants on certain jobs—mending the ancient walls dividing one field from another, for instance, or when they needed to

PLAY THE

LUCKY

CARNIVAL WHEEL

scratch-off game
and get as many as
SIX FREE GIFTS...

HOW TO PLAY:

1. With a coin, carefully scratch off the silver area at right. Then check your number against the chart below it to find out which gifts you're eligible to receive.

2. You'll receive brand-new Harlequin Presents® novels and possibly other gifts—ABSOLUTELY FREE! Send back this card and we'll promptly send you the free books and gifts you qualify for!

3. We're betting you'll want more of these heartwarming romances, so unless you tell us otherwise, every month we'll send you 8 more wonderful novels to read and enjoy. Always delivered right to your home. And always at a discount off the cover price!

4. Your satisfaction is guaranteed! You may return any shipment of books and cancel at any time. The Free Books and Gifts remain yours to keep!

NO COST! NO RISK!
NO OBLIGATION TO BUY!

FREE! 20K GOLD ELECTROPLATED CHAIN!

You'll love this 20K gold electroplated chain! The necklace is finely crafted with 160 double-soldered links, and is electroplate finished in genuine 20K gold. It's nearly ⅛″ wide, fully 20″ long—and has the look and feel of the real thing. "Glamorous" is the perfect word for it, and it can be yours FREE when you play the "LUCKY CARNIVAL WHEEL" scratch-off game!

◄ CLAIM YOUR FREE GIFTS! MAIL THIS CARD TODAY! ►

PLAY THE LUCKY
"CARNIVAL WHEEL"

Just scratch off the silver area above with a coin. Then look for your number on the chart below to see which gifts you're entitled to!

YES!

Please send me all the free books and gifts I'm entitled to. I understand that I am under no obligation to purchase any more books. I may keep the free books and gifts and return my statement marked "cancel." But if I choose to remain in the Harlequin Reader Service®, please send me 8 brand-new Harlequin Presents® novels every month and bill me the members-only low price of $2.24* each—a savings of 26 cents per book. There is no extra charge for postage and handling! I can always return a shipment at your cost and cancel at any time.

108 CIH CAPH
(U-H-P-01/90)

NAME_____
(Please Print)

ADDRESS_____APT. NO._____

CITY_____STATE_____ZIP CODE_____

39	WORTH FOUR FREE BOOKS, 20K GOLD ELECTROPLATED CHAIN AND FREE SURPRISE GIFT
15	WORTH FOUR FREE BOOKS, 20K GOLD ELECTROPLATED CHAIN
27	WORTH FOUR FREE BOOKS
6	WORTH TWO FREE BOOKS AND A FREE SURPRISE GIFT

Offer limited to one per household and not valid to current Harlequin Presents® subscribers.
*Terms and prices subject to change without notice.

© 1989 HARLEQUIN ENTERPRISES LIMITED   PRINTED IN U.S.A.

borrow the expensive pieces of machinery Josh could afford but they couldn't.

Only that morning James Allardyce had murmured something about expecting Josh round any day now to discuss a rabbit shoot.

'Oh, poor rabbits!' Prue had unwisely exclaimed, and her father had become quite excited on the subject of rabbits and their antisocial behaviour. They ate the bark off young saplings, he said, they ate his vegetables and in the spring they made havoc among newly springing wheat and barley; he reeled off a long list of reasons for the farmer's dislike of rabbits, but Prue still insisted that she loved them.

'They're sweet!'

'They're pests!' her father growled, making her laugh.

'Well, I hope you don't catch any of them,' Prue said, green eyes defiant.

She liked to get up very early in the morning and lean on her bedroom window-sill in the pale dawn light to watch the field beyond her father's garden. At that time of day it was alive with rabbits, although if Prue made the slightest sound their quick ears would hear her and they would all vanish.

How like Josh Killane to arrange to have them hunted down ruthlessly, and shot! No doubt he viewed them as pests and vermin, too. His family farm had much better land than that attached to her father's hillfarm. Josh grew crops as well as running sheep and some cattle on his valley land. He had more to lose, and far more reason to dislike rabbits!

In fact, Josh didn't show up at the farm for another two days, and when he came it wasn't to arrange a

rabbit shoot and James Allardyce wasn't at home,
anyway, he was out on the farm somewhere that
afternoon, with the local vet, checking on some sheep
giving her father anxiety.

Prue was in the farm kitchen, cooking the evening
meal, a rich lamb stew, using their own meat, and
thick with homegrown winter vegetables and herbs.
She didn't have any warning of Josh's arrival, but
then he didn't knock or ring; he just walked in
through the back door, taking her by surprise.

Face flushed, hair disorderly, she swung round,
her mouth rounding. 'Oh! You!'

His dark eyes wandered over her apron-clad figure;
she hadn't dressed for visitors, she wore no make-up
at all and under the white apron she was only
wearing a rather old and far too tight black sweater
and jeans. She stiffened under his inspection, her
hand tightening around the handle of the chopping
knife she held. Josh glanced at the hand holding the
knife, then raised one eyebrow.

'Are you planning to use that?' He managed to
invest the question with mockery.

'I was chopping parsley,' she coldly informed him.
'My father is out with the vet looking at the flock. I
don't know when he'll be back. I'll tell him you
called.' She turned her back on him and began
working again.

He didn't leave; he lounged there, very tall, very
much at his ease, dressed as casually as herself and
yet managing to make his old green tweeds look
almost glamorous. They had faded to a gentle
shabbiness which matched his surroundings but
certainly didn't betray the real wealth she knew

his family possessed. That tweed suit had probably cost the earth when it was new, but he had most likely worn it for years, and would go on doing so until it simply wore out. It had style, though; she could see it had been cut by a master tailor and the material was the best Scottish tweed.

'How's the fiancé?' he drawled.

She chopped parsley viciously. 'Fine, thank you.' She didn't want him talking about David; she didn't like the tone of voice he always used.

'A little bird told me he would be able to leave hospital a lot earlier than they thought at first; he's making such good progress.'

'We hope so.' She should have stopped chopping; she had a small mountain of parsley now. What on earth was she going to do with it all? She had only meant to chop enough to garnish the stew. Josh had addled her brains. What little bird did he mean? Had he rung the hospital to ask after David, or had her father told him? But of course he had plenty of contacts at the hospital. The Killane family had been around here since medieval times; everyone knew them and they knew everyone.

'Are you leaving then, or staying on here for a while?' Josh asked, and she put down the knife and contemplated the result of her work with impatience.

'We haven't decided yet.'

'You haven't been over to see my mother. She was hoping you would, she asked me to tell you.'

'I'm sorry, I've been very busy,' she said, sweeping the green mass of parsley into a plastic bag, which she put into the fridge to chill, slamming the fridge door shut with a little bang.

'You mean you don't want to see her!' Josh said in a brusque voice. 'I can hardly tell her that, can I?'

'And I'm very busy at the moment, too,' Prue said offhandedly. 'I'm afraid you'll have to excuse me.'

'No!'

She nearly jumped out of her skin at the way he roared that.

'I won't excuse you!' he snapped, and she backed away, staring at him nervously. 'I won't let you hurt my mother's feelings!' His face was wintry. 'If you don't visit her again while you're here, she will be hurt. She'll probably ask your father if she has done something to offend you.

'I don't want to talk about it,' Prue said, her face pale. She hadn't yet dared to talk frankly to her father, and she wasn't in a hurry to do it, either.

'I don't give a damn what you want!' Josh snarled, taking a step closer, and she backed, her whole body tense.

'I'm sure you don't!' she muttered, her green eyes fierce and defiant. 'And that's typical of your whole family—all you care about is what you want, and it doesn't bother you how many people you have to smash into the ground to get your own way! You're dinosaurs; feudal landlords out of another century, still trying to make the world work for you!'

He grabbed her shoulders, staring into her eyes. 'Feudal landlords! What the hell are you talking about? That's sheer nonsense, and you know it.'

'Get your hands off me! Don't think you can bully me!' She exerted all her strength to break his grip, but Josh tightened his fingers, shaking her furiously.

'You're thinking emotionally, Prue. Why don't you

try using your head for a change? If there was any love-affair between my mother and Jim, why haven't they got married? Why be so secretive about it? There's nothing stopping them. They're both free, they're both adults and there's no reason on earth why they shouldn't get married.'

'Maybe my father is afraid he might lose his farm,' Prue said coldly. 'After all, your mother isn't the owner of the Killane estate—you are, aren't you? If you disapproved, you could take the tenancy away without needing to give a reason.'

He laughed shortly. 'I wouldn't do a thing like that?'

'That's what you say now, but my father may still be afraid to take the risk.'

'He can't care much about my mother if all that he thinks about is his farm!'

'He's lived there all his life! And perhaps she is afraid, too. She may prefer the status quo, to go on as they have been for years, meeting in secret, rather than having a big family upset.'

'You don't know for certain that any of this is true! You only have your mother's word for it, and she was hardly a reliable witness.'

Prue paled, staring at him with bitter dislike. 'Until I came here, I only had my mother's word, but I've seen it for myself, and I'm convinced she was right.'

'What have you seen?' Josh asked.

'Love,' she said huskily.

Josh's fingers dug into her. 'What?' he ground out between his teeth.

'Do you know what the word means?' she asked, and he glowered at her; eyes like black, hot coal, a red light glowing deep within them.

'I know what it means—but do you? Would you recognise it if you saw it, or are you just imagining all this?'

'Why do you keep asking me these questions? Ask your mother. It's her we're talking about.'

'Is it?' His mouth twisted, hard and pale. 'Sure we aren't talking about you?'

Prue was not going to take that. 'Don't try to change this into another attack on me! I'm not standing trial here. You asked me why I didn't like your mother, and I was honest with you.'

'I don't think you're even honest with yourself!'

'Well, snap!' she hurled at him, and Josh glared at her for a second, then jerked her violently towards him, his mouth coming down in suffocating possession. Prue felt her heartbeat quicken to a sickening speed; she was shaking with a helpless reaction which was neither pain nor pleasure but an inextricable entwining of the two, and she hated that feeling, hated him, too. She had to get away, had to stop him, or she would go crazy, and she fought him, her body straining to escape, but it wasn't her struggle that freed her. It was a sound; a voice, an exclamation.

'Hello? Anyone in? I was . . . Oh!'

Josh lifted his head, face darkly flushed, breathing thickly, a dazed expression in his eyes as he looked round.

Prue broke away as his hands loosened their grip. She swung round to face the back door, which had opened.

Lynsey Killane stood there, staring, mouth open,

eyes very big and wide. She looked shocked, horrified.

Prue wished the ground would open up and swallow her.

CHAPTER SIX

'SORRY, I knocked, but nobody answered,' Lynsey said in a high-pitched voice.

'I won't be a minute!' said Josh, frowning.

'That was what you said when you came in here—and you've been gone nearly a quarter of an hour! It's cold and I'm getting frozen, and I'm bored stiff, so hurry up!' Lynsey gave them both a twisted little smile. 'Whatever you're doing can wait, can't it?' she murmured in a tone that sent a new wave of hot blood to Prue's face, then she vanished like a rabbit going back down a burrow.

The door banged behind her, and Josh stared across the room at where his sister had been standing. He said something angry under his breath; Prue was glad she didn't quite catch the words.

'Her face . . .' she groaned.

'Take no notice of Lynsey!' Josh said roughly. 'Don't you remember your own teens? There's nobody as censorious as an adolescent!'

Prue wasn't comforted by that thought. 'It was so embarrassing!' she muttered.

'Oh, for heaven's sake!' erupted Josh, black-browed. 'Don't make such a song and dance about it! The way you're carrying on, anyone would think Lynsey had caught us in bed together!'

Prue went crimson, and he eyed her ironically.

'What if she thinks . . .? I mean, she might . . . and if she tells anyone . . .' Prue stammered.

'If you were a little more coherent I might know what the hell you're gibbering about!' he drawled.

She repeated sharply, 'What if Lynsey tells someone what she saw?'

'She won't!'

'How can you be so sure?'

'I know my sister, and, anyway, I'll have a word with her and make quite certain that she doesn't talk about it.'

'I suppose you mean you'll bully her into doing what she's told!' Prue said with a sudden sympathy for the younger girl, and he gave her a narrow-eyed glare.

'I don't bully my little sister, any more than I bully you. Stop inventing fantasies for yourself.'

'Hadn't you better go?' she pointedly asked, turning away. 'Lynsey is still waiting, and heaven only knows what she thinks is happening in here! When you talk to her, you might make it clear that there's nothing going on between you and me!'

'After what she just saw?' he enquired softly, and she kept her back to him to hide the high colour in her face.

'Tell her you made a casual pass at me, but it didn't mean anything!'

'When I make a pass at a woman, it always means something,' he said. 'It means I fancy her.'

Prue bit her lip. So he fancied her, did he? She ought to be furious, resent the attitude that let him think he only had to reach out to get what he fancied, but although she was angry she couldn't help a secret little jab of pleasure. It was flattering, after all, to know Josh's pass had meant more than a passing impulse.

'Well . . . please, tell your sister to forget what she saw!' she pleaded.

'I might,' he drawled. 'And then again, I might not.'

'Oh, don't be so maddening!' Prue felt like hitting him again; except that from now on she meant to keep her distance at all times. She was never going to give Josh Killane another chance to lay a finger on her!

'If you want me to do you a favour, you'll have to promise to do one for me,' he said, smiling, and she eyed him suspiciously.

'What?'

'I want your promise that you'll come and see my mother, and make friends with her.'

Prue was faced with a dilemma. The last thing she wanted was to get to know his mother any better! But she had hated the way his sister had looked—that incredulous, shocked face! It had made Prue feel about two inches high. Josh had to talk to Lynsey, explain . . .

'You will make Lynsey see that she mistook what was going on? You'll tell her that we were quarrelling, not . . . not . . .'

'Making love?' he softly suggested; she looked at him with intense dislike.

'Yes. Tell her that it wasn't what . . . what it might . . . have looked like,' she muttered uncomfortably.

'I'll do my best,' he said, his smile sardonic. 'I'll lie to my sister if you'll be nice to my mother? Do we have a deal?'

'You won't have to lie to Lynsey!' Prue burst out, resentfully. 'It's the truth—we were fighting . . . not . . .'

'Not?' he silkily asked.

'Not making love!' she reluctantly got out. 'Tell her we were fighting.'

He narrowed his eyes at her, a mocking light in them. 'I love the way you fight!'

Prue ground her teeth, but resisted the instinct to retaliate. He watched her and waited, then laughed.

'So we have a deal?' he insisted, forcing her to say it.

'All right,' she muttered.

Her capitulation was not enough, it seemed. 'When will you visit my mother?' he demanded, and she turned on him, blazing with resentment, her hands screwed into fists at her sides.

'I don't know—some time tomorrow, OK?'

'Come for tea.'

'Oh, all right! Now, will you just go away and leave me in peace?'

'You have a hair-trigger temper, don't you?' he commented, as if curious about her, and her green eyes leapt with rage.

'That's right, and you're pushing it to the limit, Mr Killane! Get out, will you?'

He wandered to the back door. 'You know, you could learn a lot from my mother.'

She laughed scornfully. 'I doubt it.'

'She has good manners and a kind heart,' Josh said quietly; and then he was gone, leaving her flushed and oddly hurt. He had implied that she had neither good manners nor a kind heart, and his dark eyes had made her flinch.

Prue went back to her cooking, arranging scrubbed potatoes on a baking rack to pop them into the oven. Her father liked baked potatoes; they would be the perfect accompaniment to the lamb stew's richness.

How dared Josh talk to her like that? He barely knew her; it was unfair to make wounding personal remarks which were quite unanswerable. You couldn't yell back that you did have good manners, so there! Or insist that you had a kind heart, damn him, whatever he might think!

She finished her preparations for the evening meal, then went up to wash and change into something pretty before her father got home. He liked her to make an effort for him—she enjoyed seeing the way his face lit up when he came into the house to find her waiting for him, music playing on the stereo, flowers in vases, the smell of good food in the air.

It was a very long time since James Allardyce had had anything approaching a home life, and he was enjoying his daughter's company.

Prue was enjoying being with him, too. At first, while he was out, she had found little to do, because Betty Cain kept everything in the house scrupulously clean and, Prue soon realised, would resent any attempt she made to help. Perhaps she was afraid of losing her job? It wouldn't be surprising. There wasn't much work to be found around here.

Not that she was unfriendly, but one of her favourite phrases was 'I keep myself to myself!' Betty Cain was no gossip and never had time, so she said, to talk to Prue.

It wouldn't be difficult for a stranger to guess that a man had been living here alone. The rooms were spotless and tidy, and her father had taken the trouble to add a few touches to welcome her home—vases of autumn flowers, a few pictures, large and cheerful fires. She had thought, at first, that it was wonderful to find the house just as she remembered it, but now that she had had time to look more closely she saw the shabbiness, the faded materials of curtains and upholstery, the worn carpets and rugs. She felt the chill on the air in the upper storey, the unlived-in feel of most rooms, the sadness of a house which was often empty, nd she became increasingly determined to turn this shell of a house into a real home while she was here.

Her father came in late, glowing from his battle with the moorland wind, apologising. 'I'm sorry, love, we tramped further than we'd intended, and we stopped off at Charlie Ruddock's place for a chat and a drink.'

'Just one?' she asked tartly, and he looked sheepish.

'Well, we might have had a couple, but no more than that, Prue! When we saw how late it had got, Charlie drove us home. I hope the dinner's not charred to cinders!'

'Nearly,' she said, pretending to be annoyed, then

smiled, relenting. 'But never mind. Go and wash and get out of your muddy things.'

He was in thick woollen socks, having left his boots in the little porch at the side of the house where he kept them. He grinned at her, and padded off upstairs, while Prue began to serve up the evening meal.

The scent of lamb and herbs filled the kitchen and when Jim Allardyce returned he sniffed appreciatively. 'Eh, that smells great, lass! Looks marvellous, too! Baked potatoes! I'm very partial to a good baked potato.' He sat down and gazed over the table at all the food. 'What's that in the jug, then?'

'Sour cream with chives, Dad. For the baked potatoes.'

'Oh, aye? Chives from our own herb patch? Parsley, too! Your mother laid out the herb garden, you know, years ago, when we were first wed! She pestered me for months till I set aside some ground, then she sowed packets of seeds—I'd no idea what she had in there until it started coming up. All sorts, she'd bought, and a fair lot of it came up; beginner's luck, I told her. First bit of gardening she'd ever done, and she had no interest in any more. I've kept it going since she left, though I didn't use the herbs much, I'm afraid. I'm happy enough with a salad or a chop with a few vegetables, I don't often bother with any refinements. I'm not fussy about my food.'

'Well, I hope you'll like this!' Prue took the lid off the heavy earthenware casserole dish which she had placed in the centre of the table, and began to dish up the lamb stew. 'Josh Killane was here,' she said, placing her father's plate in front of him.

'Was he looking for me? Did you tell him where I was?'

'Yes. He was in a hurry, he had his sister with him.' Prue served herself lamb, took a baked potato and a little sour cream. 'He asked me to visit his home again tomorrow,' she said casually, not looking up.

Her father's voice had a husky note. 'And shall you?'

'Yes, I'm asked for tea—will you come?'

James Allardyce hesitated, then shook his head. 'No, you go by yourself this time, lass.'

Prue wished he had agreed to come, but perhaps it would be easier for both her and Lucy Killane if her father was not present, so she said nothing, and her father took his first mouthful of the stew and closed his eyes, savouring the flavour. Prue watched, amused. He took some more and ate, then smiled at her.

'Where did you learn to cook like that?'

'I've been living alone in a flat in Sydney for ages. I had to learn how to cook, or starve, and, since I was the one who had to eat whatever I made, I learnt how to cook well while I was about it.'

'Same with me,' James Allardyce said. 'But I'm not as ambitious as you are, a chop or a steak will do for me. And I eat out from time to time, of course.'

Did he eat out with Lucy Killane? she wondered. Did he often visit her home? And if he did, how come Josh Killane pretended to be so unaware of any intimate relationship between her father and his mother?

Prue didn't believe that anyone could be blind to the way they looked at each other. Josh Killane was a liar—but why did he lie? She did not understand his motive, but perhaps he was hoping that if he pretended not to know how they felt about each other he might stop them marrying?

She visited David in the morning and found him sitting up in a chair beside the bed, reading a murder story with a violent cover; a blonde in a bath with a knife in her chest.

'Great plot, this!' said David, after she had kissed him and sat down. 'It's the best of those you brought me.'

She looked at the cover again. 'I didn't buy that one!'

David looked at the author's name. 'Oh, no,' he said. 'I borrowed it from someone.' He pushed the book under his pillow and leaned back, yawning a little. 'Talk to me; I'm bored. How's life on the farm? Anything exciting happen in the haystacks lately?'

'Idiot,' she said, laughing, but thought that he looked very flushed—was his temperature still high?

She told him she had rung his parents, and they had been very cheerful. They had sent all sorts of loving messages, and David listened to them, smiling.

'And you didn't tell them about my lung?'

She shook her head. 'How is it now?'

'Doing fine. I think the surgeon's got a swelled

head over the way I'm healing. I told him it was my tough Australian skin that was responsible, but he seems to think it's all his doing.'

'Poor man, I'm sorry for him, having to put up with you teasing him like that,' said Prue, but David's high spirits were a good omen. He was definitely well on the way to recovery, in spite of that flush, or were his bright eyes and frenetic chatter more a symptom of fever than of good health?

She didn't tell David she was going to tea with the Killanes. It slipped her mind until after she left the ward, but she was relieved that she hadn't mentioned it because David might ask about Josh Killane and she didn't know what to say about the man. Her feelings were becoming quite explosive and it would startle David if she betrayed that.

It startled her at times. She was disturbed by the way she kept thinking about Josh, even though she hated him—hated everything about him, from his wild good looks and that rakishly insolent air to his feudal attitudes towards everyone who came within his orbit.

Mind you, his whole family seemed to have the same attitudes. They really thought they were a breed set apart, those Killanes. Centuries of arrogant possession had made them like that, and it infuriated Prue—especially the way Josh rode over the land in the valley with an air of being master of all he surveyed.

Look at the way he took domineering decisions on everything—from who should mend one of the local drystone walls to whether she should have tea with his mother!

Josh assumed too much—and that included something which seemed to come close to being droit de seigneur! He made love to her with disturbing assurance, and Prue despised herself for letting it happen. She must make sure that Josh never got another chance to do that to her!

She had asked her father a few casual questions about Josh's private life without getting any clear answers, and she dared not seem too inquisitive in case her curiosity was misunderstood, but she couldn't help wondering if Josh made passes at every woman he met!

How on earth could she ask her father that, though? She certainly couldn't ask Josh. She would just have to pick up any clues she could, and again she regretted the fact that Betty Cain was so reluctant to talk. If Betty had been the chatty type, Prue might have picked up all the local gossip. The Killanes were the most important family for miles; most local people were probably fascinated by them and their affairs, especially their love-affairs.

It was bad luck that the woman who worked for her father should be so taciturn. Only that morning, she had said to her father, 'Betty doesn't say much, does she?' and James Allardyce had laughed, shaking his head.

'Why do you think I have her here? She doesn't spread scandal about my affairs, and one look at her and nobody thinks there's anything immoral going on betwixt me and her.'

She chuckled at that idea. 'No, I don't suppose they do!'

Her father took her to lunch near the hospital, in a pretty little restaurant with red and white checked curtains and tablecloths. The food was home-cooked and excellent; Prue had soup followed by a vegetable casserole topped with grated cheese, her father had the roast of the day, beef, with Yorkshire pudding. He had a plum pie dessert, too, but Prue skipped that and just had coffee.

Her father had nodded to several other customers who kept staring across the little restuarant at their table.

'They're wondering where I picked up the pretty girl half my age!' James Allardyce said complacently, winking at her.

They probably knew she was his daughter, thought Prue. She was beginning to know these people! Gossip moved at the speed of light. A secret whispered at one end of the valley at breakfast had reached the other end by lunch time; no doubt wildly distorted!

Did they all know, or at least guess, about her father and Lucy Killane? And if not, how on earth had the two of them kept their affair a secret for so many years? Or was it simply that everyone took their relationship for granted after so long? Had time made it respectable?

Her father dropped her off half a mile from the Killane house. He had wanted to drive her all the way there, but Prue was early and preferred to walk the rest of the way, to arrive exactly on time.

'Sky looks nasty,' her father said, glancing upwards at the mass of cloud moving their way.

'It won't rain before I get there!' Prue said firmly, and he shrugged.

'Maybe,' he conceded. 'Give us a ring and I'll come and fetch you after tea.' He re-started his engine, then looked at her a little pleadingly. 'Enjoy yourself,' he said, but what he really meant was . . . be nice to Lucy Killane!

She smiled without promising and he drove on. Prue was in no hurry to cover the half a mile of meandering lane. She walked slowly, admiring the sculpted contour of the green and brown hills which made up the skyscape; the line of them rather like the outline of a woman lying down, the proud peak of a breast here, then the deep hollow of the waist in a green valley, rising softly to the smoothly undulating hip, and all of them cut clear and sharp against the sky which was gathering clouds; grey, misty, thickening with rain.

Closer at hand the countryside was starker: the rough pasture veined with grey drystone walls, sheep ambling in them, very few trees and most of them bare black skeletons rattling in the rising wind. Thorn trees bent in agonised attitudes from a lifetime of the prevailing wind; all one way, their long fingers scratching the sky. The colours here were all quiet, muted, with the faded harmony of the furniture in her father's house.

She stopped to watch a ewe scrambling up the wall, only to tumble back again. They were always escaping on to the road, she knew from her father. 'Stupid creatures, sheep,' he said, every time he got a call that some of his sheep were straying, or had had some sort of accident. 'I don't know why I don't just give up on them and breed budgerigars!'

Prue didn't look at her watch until she was within sight of the Killane house, and then she was surprised to see how long it had taken her to walk the half-mile from where her father had dropped her. She was going to be late! She quickened her steps just as a car came shooting down the drive, heading her way. Recognising it, Prue felt a jab of pure nerves. She had hoped Josh would be out, but this was his car.

He pulled up with a squeal of brakes and leaned over to open the passenger door. 'Get in!'

Prue resented the brusque tone. 'I can walk, there's no need to stop for me. You're obviously in a hurry to get somewhere.'

'I was in a hurry to find you!' he snapped. 'As you hadn't arrived, I rang your home and your father told me he had dropped you at the crossroads and you should have got to our house by now. Where the hell have you been?'

'I was enjoying the view!'

'And in no hurry to arrive!' he accused.

'I just didn't notice the time!'

'Is this the way you keep your promises? To the letter, but not abiding by the spirit?'

She bridled. 'What about you? Have you kept your promise? Have you talked to your sister?'

'Yes,' he said, tight-lipped.

Prue frowned at his glowering expression. 'Did you convince her?'

He gestured impatiently. 'Look, get in, will you? My engine is idling away here, wasting fuel. We can talk as we drive.'

She reluctantly climbed into the car; and Josh at once reversed and drove back to the house at around sixty miles an hour.

'Lynsey was in a very difficult mood when I talked to her,' he said, staring straight ahead.

'Well, that seems to be her usual mood, so I'm not surprised,' Prue said, grimacing. 'But did she seem to believe you?'

'Frankly, no,' Josh said tersely.

'What did you say to her? Did you tell her . . .'

'I told her what you wanted me to tell her—a lot of lies!' said Josh.

'Oh, well, if you weren't even trying to sound convincing——' Prue scornfully said.

Josh slammed on his brakes and Prue nearly went through the windscreen. When she had got her breath back and stopped shaking, she flung round to glare hatred at him. 'You maniac! You scared the living daylights out of me. Isn't one car crash enough for you?'

He showed her his teeth in a wolfish snarl. 'Now, look, I kept my side of the deal—I talked to my sister, I said all the things you asked me to say. Can I help it if she wouldn't buy it?'

Prue was sure it was somehow his fault; if only she could prove it! 'What did she actually say to you, though?'

'Not much.'

Prue didn't like something in his dark eyes; an irony, a hidden amusement.

'She must have said something!' she insisted and Josh considered her, his head to one side and his mouth twisting.

'She laughed.'

Prue's green eyes opened wide. 'Laughed?' she whispered.

He nodded. 'In my face!'

It was bad news. Prue didn't like it. If Lynsey had laughed in his face, it meant that she hadn't believed a word he said.

'Oh, dear,' Prue said.

'Inadequate,' said Josh, and then he laughed; laughed loudly before he started driving on while Prue sat beside him, quivering with rage.

As she got out of the car Mrs Killane appeared on the steps, her face concerned. 'Josh found you—good! We were worried when Jim told us that you should have got here long ago! Did you get lost?'

'I'm sorry,' Prue stiffly said, joining her. 'I was just wandering along in a daydream.' She pretended not to feel the cold stab of Josh's eyes. 'You have such beautiful views,' she added rather defiantly, and Mrs Killane gave her a brilliant smile, nodding.

'Haven't we? I've often got lost in a daydream, looking at the hills.'

She swept Prue into the house, talking about her favourite local beauty spots, then smiled at her a little shyly. 'I'm so glad you could come,' she said. 'Lynsey is out, and Josh has to go into town to buy something, so it will just be you and me. I hope you won't be bored.'

Deeply relieved to find that Josh wasn't going to be present, Prue said, 'Of course not!' following Mrs

Killane into a sunny room.

'How's your fiancé?' Mrs Killane asked, gesturing to her to sit down in one of the deep, comfortable armchairs on either side of a low table which was already laid for tea with thin sandwiches, scones and small home-made cakes.

'Much better, thank you. I'm hoping he will be out of hospital in a week.' Prue was finding it easier to talk to Lucy Killane than she had expected; partly because they were alone and she didn't have to keep remembering the reason why she should dislike her. Josh's absence oddly made it easier, too. Whenever he was around, Prue found herself charged with angry engery, but now she felt peaceful and at ease.

'Oh, that is good,' said Lucy Killane. 'Such a pity, to have an accident when you're on holiday, and having come all that way! It must have been very expensive for you, this trip.'

'We came economy,' Prue admitted. 'Neither of us had much money.' David had some savings, and she was using some of the money she had inherited from her mother; it had seemed a fitting way to spend it, discovering her roots and mending fences with her father.

Mrs Killane sat down and talked for several minutes about holidays, then got up, saying, 'I'll make the tea now, excuse me for a moment.'

While she was out of the room, Prue wandered around, looking out of the window at a rose garden where the wind rustled last, defiant blooms; they had a melancholy look and Prue sighed, turning back to the room and went to inspect a bookcase full of well-read books. It was always fascinating to see what other people read, and she soon realised the books did not belong to Josh. There were some cookery books, gardening books, but most were novels. Prue recognised many of her own favourite authors: childhood classics like Alice or *The Wind in the Willows*, mingling with more adult writers like Jane Austen, the Brontës, Georgette Heyer, Angela Thirkell, Jilly Cooper.

Mrs Killane came back with a tray on which were arranged a teapot, covered with a hand-knitted teacosy, a sugar bowl and matching jug in flower-sprigged bone china, cups from the same set and a tea-strainer over a small matching bowl.

Prue quickly turned, a book in her hand, making an apologetic face. 'I'm sorry, I couldn't resist . . .'

'Not at all!' Mrs Killane said eagerly. 'I'm just the same, if I see books in someone's house I can't help taking a peek. It's as good as a character reference, isn't it? You know so much about someone from what they read.' She poured the tea and Prue sat down again, accepting a cup of tea and one of the tiny, wafer-thin sandwiches filled with a crisp medley of salad chopped up very small.

'Did you make these?' she asked, taking a home-made scone next and refusing any of the thick, whipped cream, although she took home-made strawberry jam.

'Made from our own strawberries,' Mrs Killane told her, and said, 'Yes, I love to cook.'

'I saw you had quite a few cookery books.' Prue

smiled. 'And that you like romantic novels!'

'Do you?'

'Love them!' Prue said. 'Which do you prefer—*Jane Eyre* or *Wuthering Heights*?'

'Oh, heavens! What a question,' Mrs Killane said, leaning back to think it over. 'Well . . .' she began, while Prue took a bite of the slice of chocolate swiss roll that had just been placed on her plate.

They talked quite freely after that; keeping on neutral subjects which offered no danger zones. Books were the easiest—they were each happiest talking about their favourites, and it excluded all mention of either James Allardyce or Josh.

He walked into the room an hour later, and they both turned laughing countenances towards him. Prue stopped laughing when she saw Josh, but his mother beamed.

'You're back, then! Did you get the tools you wanted?'

'Some of them,' he said, his dark eyes glinting on Prue's cooling expression.

Prue hated the smooth voice, the edge of derision it carried. She looked at her watch and got up hurriedly.

'I must be going. Thank you for tea, Mrs Killane . . .'

'Call me Lucy, Prue, and thank you for making my afternoon so pleasant. We must talk about our favourite authors again soon.'

'I'll run you back,' Josh said in the hall, but Prue shook her head firmly.

'I'd rather walk, thanks. I need the exercise. See you again, Mrs . . . Lucy!'

Mrs Killane looked anxiously at the sky. 'It's almost dark, and it looks like rain.'

'I'll drive her,' Josh said, but Prue began to walk off down the drive, bristling at the way he talked about her as if she was a child or a half-wit. But then, that was how he saw women—half-witted children who needed his feudal mix of bullying and protection. She had seen the way he ordered his sister around, and he had tried the same approach with her any number of times now. Prue wasn't having it.

'Oh, suit yourself!' he snapped, his engine roaring as he shot past. She watched his tail-lights disappear in the gloom and felt stupid. It was a long walk back to the farm, and it might have been more sensible to accept a lift, but she just couldn't face the prospect of being alone with him again. Last time, she had promised herself it would never happen again; she was avoiding him in future. She was going to keep that promise.

Thank God she and David would soon be on their way. She would miss her father badly, she loved the farm and the valley and the stark, breath-taking landscape she saw each morning from her bedroom window. But she had to get away from Josh Killane.

She had been walking for ten minutes when the rain started; little drops at first, then a torrential downpour which rapidly reduced her to a sodden rag—her red hair darkened, flattened against her skin like a skull cap, her clothes soon saturated and her shoes began to let water in at every seam.

There was nowhere to take shelter; she had to

trudge on, her head down into the wind and rain, praying now that Josh would turn round and come back for her. He must know that she was almost drowning, fighting with a wind blowing right into her face and trying to blow her back to Killane House—surely he would come to her rescue?

She grimaced, staring into the rain-slashed night. Why should he? She had refused a lift offhandedly, said she wanted to walk—why should he come back for her?

When the headlights cut through the darkness, she gave a sigh of relief and slowed, looking into the car.

It wasn't Josh; it was someone else, a stranger, thickset and slightly balding. 'Bad night to be out walking,' he said in a strong Yorkshire accent. 'Want a lift?'

Prue hesitated, trying to sum him up from his face. 'Thank you,' she said uncertainly. He looked OK, and anyway she was wet and exhausted after the battle with the weather.

She got into the passenger seat and he drove on, asking, 'Where shall I drop you?'

She told him and he gave her a quick look. 'Oh, you're Jim Allardyce's girl, are you? I heard you were home. Bet they don't have storms like this in Australia.'

She laughed. Australian weather could be far worse, in fact, but she knew better than to say so. She was relieved that he knew her father; at least she hadn't been picked up by a stranger. She asked him his name and where he lived, and by the time he had finished telling her they were at the end of her father's drive, and a car was turning out of it, blocking the entrance.

'Probably Jim out looking for you,' said the other man, but Prue took one glance and knew it wasn't. The driver realised it too, a second later. 'No, it's Josh Killane,' he said, and then Josh leapt out of his car and came round to pull open the door beside Prue.

'I was just coming to get you,' he said, then threw a brusque nod to the driver. 'Thanks, Bob. Good of you to stop.'

'Thank you very much,' Prue said to the driver, smiling at him.

'That's OK,' he said, and she got out. Josh slammed the door behind her, grabbed her by the waist with peremptory force and rushed her across to his own car. She found herself being crammed into it roughly, and then the door closed and Josh came round and dived in beside her.

The other car drove off but Josh did not start his engine; he turned to glare at her, temper making his face tight.

'Have you met him before?'

'No,' she said. 'Can we go? I'm dripping all over your upholstery.'

'You got into a total stranger's car and let him drive off with you?'

'I was getting wet, and I still am wet, very wet. I'd like to go home and change into some dry clothes, please.' She added the 'please' as an afterthought, reluctantly, because the way he was looking at her and breathing hard was making her nervous, and she felt it might be wiser to placate him a little.

'You refused my offer of a lift, then got into a stranger's car?'

'Are you having trouble understanding the obvious?' Prue asked aggressively, since placation had not worked.

'You're the most stupid, the most irritating female I've ever met!' he snarled, and Prue decided she did not like being called that, so she snarled back.

'Don't you yell at me! People keep telling me about this mythical being they call a blunt Yorkshire man; I suppose you're it? Well, I've had about enough of your insults and personal remarks; so either drive me home right away or I'm getting out again. I'd rather swim home that sit here while you pull me to pieces.'

'I'm tempted to let you walk, too!'

Prue reached for the door-handle, although she dreaded the idea of going back out into that rain.'

'But I left you to walk back earlier,' he bit out. 'And found myself coming back to look for you, so this time I'll make sure you get home.'

Josh started the car so fast that she was thrown sideways to collide with him. Her nerve-ends were jittery as she sat up again, avoiding his angry stare. Josh drove to the farmhouse at high speed. He braked just as suddenly and swung round to face Prue, his eyes fierce and very black.

'Don't!' she whispered, shaking helplessly. She had never been so afraid in her life. Josh sat there, staring into her face, then he turned away, put both hands on the steering wheel, his whole body stiff with tension.

Prue got out of the car and ran away as if pursued by a deadly enemy.

CHAPTER SEVEN

OVER the next week, time seemed to drag. The hire car had been repaired and she had that back, so she was able to drive herself to the hospital each day to see David, but for the rest of each day she had very little to do. She tried to keep busy, going out with her father if he was working near the house, to watch him and give a hand with whatever he was doing; or, if it wasn't possible for her to go with him, she worked indoors, cooking or preserving some of the luscious autumn fruits she found around the farm—blackberries and sloes and crab apples in the hedgerows; and, in the orchard, apples and pears.

She did not see Josh all week, but Lucy Killane came over to see her one day, bringing grapes grown on an indoor vine at Killane House. They were a little sharp but had quite a palatable flavour. Lucy Killane said she made wine with them most years. The vine had been growing in the hothouse for years; it had been planted by her husband when they were first married.

Prue was able to see her father's unguarded face when Lucy first appeared; his eyes lit up and his mouth curved in a tenderness that made her absolutely certain that he loved Lucy. She watched Lucy talking to him, but wasn't quite so sure about how she felt—fondness, yes, that was there, but was there more than that?

'Has your daughter gone back to college?' she asked, and Lucy sighed, shaking her head.

'Not yet. She can be very difficult.'

Prue could believe that! She hadn't seen much of Lynsey, but she had a shrewd idea that the other girl had a strong will and something of her brother's tenacity.

'Is she still quarrelling with Josh?' asked James Allardyce, and Lucy gave him a wry smile.

'Afraid so!'

'Josh should be more understanding!' Prue's father said, and Prue laughed.

'And pigs should fly!'

Lucy gave her an astounded glance, and her father looked shocked.

'Prue!'

'I'm sorry, but it's true . . . expecting Josh to be understanding is as realistic as asking a pig to fly. He doesn't understand women and he never will.'

'Don't you think so?' Josh's mother said, staring at her with a thoughtful expression.

'Well, I don't expect you to agree with me, you are his mother, after all,' Prue said defiantly. 'But it doesn't surprise me that he tries to push his sister around, or that she quarrels with him all the time. If I were her, so would I!'

'You quarrel with Josh a lot?' his mother asked, and Prue went a little pink, her green eyes restlessly moving away from Lucy Killane's curious gaze.

'If he tries to ridge roughshod over me, yes! Maybe it's because I grew up in another country, with different rules and attitudes—but I won't put up with a man giving me orders.'

'Oh, dear,' Lucy said, smiling. 'I can see Josh has rubbed you up the wrong way.'

When she had gone, James Allardyce said to Prue rather huskily, 'I'm so glad you and Lucy are getting on better now. I was sure you would like her when you got to know her.'

Prue smiled, sympathy in her eyes. She was sure now that her father loved Lucy Killane, and almost sure that Lucy did not feel quite the same way about him. Her affection was sisterly, Prue suspected. She was fond of him, but had never been in love. My mother was wrong, Prue thought; well, half wrong, anyway! But would that have been any comfort to her mother, since it was true that James Allardyce did love the other woman?

'I like Lucy very much,' she said gently, and her father glowed with pleasure.

'Good.' He gave her a faintly mischievous look. 'And maybe one day you'll start to like Josh, too!'

Prue stopped smiling and glowered; green eyes glittering in her flushed face. 'That is never going to happen!'

David was due to leave the hospital very soon. The following day, Prue stayed within earshot of the telephone in case she was given the word to come and collect him. His specialist was visiting him that morning, and the ward sister had told Prue that he might decide that David was fit enough to go home, so Prue had packed a case with clothes for David, and taken it into the hospital the previous day. If he was given the go-ahead, he could be dressed and waiting by the time Prue arrived to pick him up.

James Allardyce was working in the field nearest the house that morning. If the call came, all she had to do was yell to her father then hurry and and drive to the hospital to pick David up.

She was feeling oddly edgy as she waited for the phone to ring. On the one hand, she couldn't wait for David to rejoin her; she was aching to get on with their holiday, and then with their life together. She had loved him for a long time, nothing could ever change that.

On the other hand, though, she would miss her father terribly; she loved the farm and the landscape she saw each morning when she got up; and she was rather nervous about going away with David. It would be crazy to say he seemed like a stranger; but something had happened to them both since the crash. His weeks in hospital had separated them somehow. David had lived through an experience she hadn't shared, and at the same time she had been reliving the childhood he hadn't known, rediscovering her father, realising she belonged here, after all. She had found out a lot about herself in the process, too.

She had seen David every day, of course—but she had increasingly felt like a stranger; they had talked in a cheerful way, but so politely, a distance between them, some barrier she didn't understand. Prue frowned, telling herself fiercely that when they were together again, and far away from here, they would get back together again. They still loved each other just the way they always had! She couldn't imagine marrying anyone but David—why, their friends had always said that theirs was a marriage made in heaven, fated!

Prue made herself some coffee and stared at the phone, willing it to ring. Betty Cain had whisked around the house and left; everything was tidy and she had nothing to do but wait.

Fifteen minutes later, she was washing up her coffee-cup and spoon in an obsessive need to do something to pass the time when Josh walked into the kitchen from the garden, wearing well-washed old blue jeans which fitted him like a glove, and a skin-tight black ribbed sweater over an old grey shirt.

Prue looked over her shoulder, with a stifled little gasp, her eyes restlessly skating over his lean figure, surprised by a faintly dishevelled look about him. He was usually so well groomed: hair smoothly brushed, nails immaculate, clothes exactly right for whatever occasion he was attending. Today, she sensed that he was in too much of a temper to bother how he looked—he was probably a hazard to anyone who was foolish enough to cross his path, too, but he was here, and short of running away there was no way she could avoid him, so she nodded warily instead.

Josh nodded to her, his brows black as night, his eyes blacker.

'Dad's in Lark Meadow, if you want him,' she said in a hurry, hoping he would go in search of her father.

'I came to see you.' His tone was uncompromising

and she wondered nervously what was wrong now.
Had his mother repeated what she'd said about him?
Oh, good grief! Prue inwardly groaned—I hope not!
She could have sworn that Lucy Killane wouldn't do
that.

'I'm sorry,' she said, drying her hands and trying
to look busy. 'I haven't got time to talk, I'm off any
minute to pick up David at the hospital!'

'No, you're not!' His peremptory voice put her
back up; she threw the towel down and glared at
him.

'Whatever you want to say will have to wait!' she
muttered. 'They'll be ringing me any time now, and
then I'll be driving to the hospital.'

'Your fiancé has already left,' Josh said, his eyes
hard and watchful.

She stared at him blankly.

'What?'

'He left two hours ago.'

Prue looked at the door, as if expecting David to
walk through it any moment.

'No!' Josh said in a flat voice. 'He isn't here.'

'Where is he, then? What's happened? Why did he
leave the hospital without letting me know . . .' Her
voice died away as she stared into Josh's furious
eyes, and she became afraid.

'I don't know where he is—yet!' Josh said through
his teeth. 'But I'll find him—and when I do, I'll break
his neck!'

The violence in his voice made Prue flinch away
from him, her green eyes huge and troubled. 'What
are you talking about?'

'He's run off,' Josh said hoarsely. 'And he's taken

my sister with him!'

Frozen, Prue whispered, 'Run off? David? But where has he gone? I don't understand what you're talking about! What has your sister got to do with David?'

'I told you,' Josh said, his dark eyes stabbing at her as if he blamed her for whatever had happened. 'They've gone off together . . . Lynsey and that bastard!'

'I don't believe you!' Prue said, but she began to feel cold, her skin lost all its colour and her eyes darkened with fear.

Josh gave a rough sigh of irritation, shrugging. 'I wish it wasn't true, too, God knows! But it is. Look, I only heard by accident—my shepherd cut his hand on a scythe early today, cutting back brambles, and his wife drove him to the hospital to have it stitched and to get tetanus jabs. When they got back, I went to their cottage to check that he was OK, and they mentioned seeing Lynsey driving away from the hospital. That rocked me, because she hadn't mentioned going to the hospital, so I asked if they were sure and they said yes, they'd know her car anywhere. It's an old banger of mine; I gave it to her for her last birthday, to help her pass her test. I'd had it for years, so they weren't likely to be mistaken.'

Prue tensely interrupted, 'But you said she left with David!'

'She did!' Josh irritably told her.

'But how could your shepherd know that? He doesn't know David.'

'He didn't know who the man was with her, he just knew there was a man in the passenger seat, but his wife, who had had to sit in the foyer while he was seeing the doctor, had seen Lynsey collect the man from one of the wards.'

'But why on earth jump to the conclusion that it was David?' Prue was disturbed, but she couldn't believe that any of this was true. After all, Lynsey had only met David once, and anyway, she was just a teenager! David wouldn't run off with some eighteen-year-old!

'I rang the hospital! They told me Henley had left with Lynsey,' Josh said harshly, and she stared at him, her stomach churning, and heard the clock ticking, heard water dripping in the kitchen sink, and outside a bird singing with melancholy persistence somewhere among the leafless wintry trees. Such small domestic sounds, yet they were like nails being driven into her flesh.

'Then she's bringing him here,' Prue said in a thin, dry voice, through lips turned white and shaky.

Josh watched her expressionlessly, shaking his head, and she picked up a flash of pity in those dark eyes, and it made her even wilder; her voice taking on an edge of desperation.

'She must be . . . they'll be here soon . . . you're crazy, jumping to conclusions . . .'

'I know most of the staff pretty well,' Josh said flatly, interrupting. 'My family built the original hospital . . .'

'I know,' she said bitterly. 'I went to school here until I was thirteen, remember? I don't need a local history lesson about how the Killanes gave the money to build the cottage hospital. They told us all about it, and told us how grateful we ought to be!'

Her very obvious lack of gratitude didn't seem to bother Josh too much, although he did give her a faintly wry glance.

'They still call one of the wards Killane,' he said. 'And I'm on several committees concerned with the day-to-day running of the place, so I knew that all I had to do was ring the head porter, Phil Maley—he knows everything that goes on in the hospital. I asked if Lynsey had arrived yet, and he cheerfully told me she'd already collected your fiancé.' Josh smiled; it wasn't a very pleasant smile and Prue winced. 'He thought I knew all about it, of course! He knows your father is my tenant and it seemed very natural that Lynsey should drive over to pick your fiancé up.'

'Well, isn't it?' Prue burst out.

Josh shook his head. 'No, that . . .'

She broke in angrily, 'Why not? Why shouldn't she have called in by chance, discovered that David could leave at once, and offered him a lift back to the farm? That must be what's happened.' Her voice picked up, she almost smiled. 'Yes, that's it! Probably, your sister is taking the long way round from the hospital . . . sightseeing . . . she may have called in somewhere else, on friends, not realising that David is still weak and should go straight to bed. I'd say that that is the most plausible explanation.'

Josh gave her a wry smile. 'Plausible maybe, but it isn't true, I'm afraid!'

'How can you possibly know?' she asked, dreading his answer.

Josh pulled a crumpled letter out of his pocket and Prue's eyes focused on it blindly, her face growing even whiter.

'Lynsey gave this to a nurse to post. When I went over to the hospital, they gave it to me.'

He held it out but Prue didn't take it, shaking her head. 'I don't want to read your letter! What does she say?'

'It wasn't addressed to me, and it isn't from Lynsey.'

'You said Lynsey gave it to a nurse to post!'

'She did, but she didn't write the letter. He did. They meant it to be posted, so that you wouldn't get it until tomorrow morning.' His mouth was cynical, distasteful. 'They wanted to make sure of getting away before anyone found out what they were planning.' He pushed the envelope at Prue, and this time she took it with trembling fingers and turned it over and over, staring down at it.

'You've opened it!'

'And read it,' said Josh coolly. 'I had to know what it said.'

'You had no right to open a letter addressed to me!'

'I was in a hurry. I didn't know what was going on, I just knew that my sister was up to something. I even wondered if you and your fiancé had both gone with Lynsey, if you were in some sort of conspiracy to spirit her away so that she didn't have to go back to university! But when I was given that letter, I realised they wouldn't be writing to you if you were going off with them, so I opened the letter and read it.'

Prue unfolded the crumpled paper and stared at David's sprawling, untidy handwriting. She was in such a state that she could hardly make out one word in three, but the word sorry leapt out at her over and over again. She read it, and lifted her head, her face stricken.

'He says they're in love . . .'

'I know, I read it, remember!' Josh interrupted impatiently.

'They're getting married right away, as soon as they can get a licence,' she said over him, as if he hadn't spoken, and then she laughed with bitter irony. 'We've been engaged for a year! For one reason or another, it was never the right time to get married, and we were quite happy to wait; after all, we had all our lives ahead of us.' She held up the letter, staring at Josh. 'But he wants to marry her at once!'

'Not if I can stop it,' Josh said, watching her tensely.

'But I don't understand any of it,' Prue said, her green eyes bewildered. 'They barely know each other! David's been in hospital ever since we got here and I've been visiting him every day. How can they be in love?'

Josh's face was dark with angry blood. 'Lynsey has been visiting him too, ever since that first time, when she took him those flowers. She obviously took one look and fell for him. My God, if I'd known I'd have packed her off to university again before her feet could touch the ground, but then she knew how I'd feel if I ever found out. She took great trouble to hide what she was up to!' Josh gave a thick groan. 'She seems to have made the running, it may not be his fault as much as hers.' The admission was reluctant, irritated, and then he burst out, 'Although how he could dump you to run off with an eighteen-year-old girl, God only knows.'

The word 'dump' made Prue wince; her pallor growing more pronounced and her green eyes all dilated pupil; black with pain.

'He was probably flattered,' Josh said, mouth twisting. 'Most men would be—Lynsey's beautiful, even if she is just a kid. Having her throwing herself at him must have turned his head, not that that excuses what he's done. He should have known better, he's years older than her, and they hardly know each other, even if she has been visiting him every day for the last couple of weeks.'

Prue had been thinking about that, and a sudden wave of violent hot colour ran up her face. 'Oh, she really meant to get him, didn't she?'

Josh shrugged, his mouth indented. 'She's the age for obsessions; for seeing things just from her own angle.'

'Don't blame her age!' Prue said bitterly. 'She's a Killane—that's why she did it!'

Josh looked at her sharply, eyes narrowed.

'She's her mother's daughter,' Prue flung at him. 'It's the same pattern, isn't it? Your mother stole my father, even though she didn't really want him at all. And David was mine, so your sister had to have him! I don't suppose this is even the first time she's gone after another girl's man. With some women it just makes it more exciting, knowing they're stealing a man from someone else. He's been very ill and he still isn't back to normal; he doesn't know what he's doing, she's bewitched him into going away with her . . . it isn't David's fault, any of this, it's hers.' She was talking in a high, shaking voice, her eyes feverish and her body trembling, and Josh was staring at her fixedly, his brows black above his black eyes.

'You're hysterical, stop talking like that!' he said curtly, but she wouldn't stop; the words kept pouring out of her in a molten lava, and she felt confused about why she was so sick and angry. She didn't know if the pain was over her father or over David, only that the echo of an old betrayal was sounding in her ears like surf in a sea shell. Talking helped her to stave off tears, so she kept talking.

'I know now how my mother felt!' she said huskily, swallowing. 'When I remember how fed up I used to get with listening to her . . . but I hadn't been there then, I didn't know!' She broke off, biting her lower lip to stop it shaking. 'I should never have come back here, but it never entered my head that I'd lose David, that it might all happen again. I remember being surprised that day she took David flowers, it seemed an odd thing to do, but I misunderstood, I thought she did it to score off me, make me feel thoughtless and stupid because I hadn't thought of giving him flowers, and all the time she had made up her mind there and then to steal him from me, the way your mother stole my father . . .'

Josh slapped her face and the wild, hoarse words stopped in a gasp. She stared at him, green eyes huge and blank for a second, then the tears welled up in them and Josh grabbed her, his arms round her, while she began to cry, shaking and sobbing.

She let him hold her, her face buried in his chest, the ribbing of his sweater pressing against her skin, although she wasn't aware of it at the time. His hand cupped the back of her head, slowly moved over her hair, gently stroking it, comforting her, while she cried out all the rage and pain which had made her close to hysterical.

She gradually stopped crying but she didn't move, her body still quivering with the hurricane of emotion which had swept through it. Face hidden against Josh's chest, she fought to control her breathing, sneaked up a hand to brush over her wet face, gave a shuddering sigh.

Then the hand stroking her hair suddenly clenched on a handful of it and pulled her head back.

'Don't!' she protested. 'That hurts!'

Josh didn't let go; his hand ruthlessly enforcing pressure, he made her look up at him, his dark eyes probing her face.

'Isn't it time you were honest with yourself?' he asked, his mouth sardonic, and she frowned, the tear-wet lashes drooping to hide her eyes from him.

'Don't you talk to me about being honest. One of your family has no business mentioning the word honesty to one of mine!'

'You don't love him!' Josh said tersely and she drew a sharp, appalled breath.

'Let go of me!' She fought him breathlessly, her hands curled into fists, punching him, and Josh had to let go of her hair, but only to put both arms around her again, making it impossible for her to get her hands free.

'You . . . you . . . Killane!' she raged. 'Stop touching me like that—I hate it!'

He put his head down close to hers and she hurriedly averted her face, but could not stop his cheek touching her own, or silence his whisper against her ear. 'No, you don't—and you don't love him, either!'

Her face burned, then went white again. 'Do you think I don't know what you're doing?' she muttered, staring at the kitchen window over his shoulder, watching the sun shine through the leafless branches of a thorn tree, and hating Josh even more than she hated his sister. 'You want me to give David up without a protest. Your little sister wants him, so I must be convinced that I never loved him. We must make it easier for Lynsey, mustn't we? She's a Killane, and the Killanes must always get what they want!'

'You must be fond of him, I'm sure you are,' said Josh coolly, ignoring her accusations. 'But love is very different, Prue—you know that, so don't lie to yourself, even if you feel you must lie to me.' His cheek was against hers, his flesh warm, his skin rougher than her own as he rubbed his face backward and forward against her cheek. She could smell the musky scent of his aftershave, and hear his breathing, feel his chest rise and fall against her breasts as his lungs drew in air and exhaled it. Their bodies were breathing in the same rhythm, their hearts beating with the same over-rapid excitement.

'Don't talk to me about love!' she broke out, angry with herself as much as him because he was getting to her, just as he always had, right from their first meeting. The violence of her reactions to him scared her as much now as it had then, and she was desperate to stop him saying any more. She didn't want to hear the things he was saying; she didn't want them to be true.

'Why not?' he asked softly, a thread of mockery in his voice, turning his head a little so that his mouth moved on her earlobe, the warmth of his breath and his lips making her shudder. 'Why mustn't I talk about love, Prue? Why are you so scared?'

'You're all the same, you Killanes, aren't you?' she said thickly, shifting her head to escape the teasing brush of his mouth.

'Sooner or later you've got to face the truth.' His lips touched her neck, as gently as a feather gliding over her skin, making her shiver. The kiss drifted slowly down her throat towards her cheek, inflicting pain and pleasure, coming closer and closer to her quivering mouth; insidious, seductive, tormenting. She tried to wriggle free but couldn't; his hands held her prisoner.

Josh was stronger and he had no scruples about using his strength. He wasn't hurting her, she almost wished he was, it would make it easier to bear, make it easier to fight. As it was, she had to force herself to struggle, to free her arms. She was struggling to free her senses, too, from the spell he was weaving around them, but she hoped he didn't know that. She would hate Josh to know he had almost beaten her.

Tensing herself from head to foot, she said furiously, 'Let go! I don't want you touching me, I don't want you kissing me or flirting with me—any of it! You're just like the rest of your family!'

He stiffened, his hands releasing her for a second and then catching hold of her again, gripping her shoulders so tightly that she winced.

'What are you accusing me of now?' he asked with a kind of weary impatience.

'Don't think you fooled me for an instant, not even at the start!' she said, her green eyes full of hate. 'You were very obvious! Once you knew I was engaged, you started chasing me, the way your little sister chased David . . . you're all the same, you Killanes—the grass is always greener on the other side of the wall! You only want what other people have!'

'That's not true,' he said, his face all angles and those dark eyes filled with angry heat, and a sort of surprise, but then he hadn't expected her to work it out, to realise why he had made passes at her even though he knew she was engaged.

'Oh, yes, it is! I suppose you thought I was too dumb to realise what you were doing? Well, I'm not! You didn't take me in, not for a second.'

'Stop talking nonsense!' Josh said, through tight lips.

'It isn't nonsense; it's the truth and it's no good denying it! Your mother flirted with my father, but she hasn't married him. You knew I was engaged, but you've flirted with me. Your sister knew David was engaged, but she flirted with him. The only difference was that David fell for it—he took it seriously and she's had to take it seriously, too. She's run off with him. But how long will it last? Will she get bored with him before they've actually fixed a wedding day?'

'What if she did?' Josh asked, his eyes narrowing on her.

'What if she did?' Prue repeated, staring back with distaste. 'Who cares, is that it? She'll have her fun, and then she'll get bored, she'll walk out on poor David, and she'll come home . . . wagging her tail behind her!' She began to laugh wildly, her eyes wide and glistening with unshed tears, and Josh watched her, his face grim.

'That wasn't what I meant! If she does leave him, will you take him back? That was what I wanted to know!'

Prue hadn't even thought of that, but she thought of it then, eyes shadowed, and knew that she wouldn't, that it was all over between her and David. She never wanted to see him again; he had humiliated her, betrayed her, just as her father had betrayed her mother. It might be David who had jilted her, but it was she who felt the shame and the guilt. She could never look him in the face again.

'Well?' Josh insisted, his eyes fixed on her face, and she pulled herself together and looked coolly at him. He was the very last person in the world she would confide in; she wasn't telling him what she was thinking, he could ask until he was blue in the face.

'Mind your own business,' she said, and got a long, searing stare before Josh turned on his heel and walked out of the kitchen into the garden. If he had slammed the door she might have felt some sort of angry triumph, but he didn't. He closed the door behind him with a quiet finality which left her feeling very cold and tired.

CHAPTER EIGHT

PRUE was too shocked to be capable of thinking clearly. When Josh had gone, she went upstairs like an automaton to pack, before her father got back. She had the hire car; she could be miles away in a few hours, and then she wouldn't have to put up with pity or sympathy from her father, she could leave all this muddle behind.

But she couldn't make up her mind, she switched plans every five minutes as she sat in her bedroom in the farmhouse, her suitcases open and her clothes strewn all over the bed. What should she do? She must decide!

Think! she told herself angrily. What should I do? Do I stay on here—or leave? And then, if she left Yorkshire, should she go off on that long-planned trip around Europe, visiting all the places she and David had dreamt about and talked about for months, but which she would be seeing all by herself now? Or should she fly straight back to Australia?

She looked at her suitcases, biting her lip. How could she go back to Sydney and her job with her old firm, see her old friends again, after David had walked out on her? It would be humiliating; they might be sympathetic to her face, but some of them would giggle behind her back, or, at the very least, whisper and gossip, seething with curiosity. She didn't know which she would hate most—the pity or the secret glee.

There was another reason why she was reluctant to go back to Australia. David would probably take Lynsey back to Sydney after they were married. Where else would they go? David's parents were there, and she and David had always planned to go back after their lengthy tour of Europe. It was quite the thing among their friends to see the world and then come home to settle down and start a family; they had never intended to stay in Europe.

She had looked forward to living close to David's parents; she was very fond of them, and that would be another bitter loss to her. She would probably never see them again. When they heard the news, they would be very upset, they would be deeply sorry for her, and angry with David for jilting her. Knowing them, she wouldn't be surprised if they chose to side with her against their own son, and she didn't want that!

She wasn't sure yet how she felt about David himself. She ought to hate him, but she couldn't. She loved David too much to hate him; nothing he did would ever alter that. She couldn't even blame him. In fact, she had a sneaking fellow feeling for him. He was another victim of the Killanes and their insidious glamour; like her father and her mother . . . and herself.

The slam of a door downstairs made her sit up; face pale and alert. Was that her father? She hadn't been expecting him home for ages yet.

'Hello? Anyone at home?'

It was a woman's voice. Lucy Killane, thought

Prue, frowning, and not answering, hoping that the older woman would go away. Josh must have told her. She must be worried about her daughter, but why had she come here? What did she want?

She wants something, you can bet on that! Prue thought cynically. Maybe she has come to soft-soap me, get me to forgive her daughter and promise not to make a scandal, cause trouble for the Killane family?

'Prue, are you there?'

Footsteps creaked on the stairs; Mrs Killane was coming up and Prue got off the bed, closed her suitcase, flung them with her clothes back into the wardrobe and shut the doors on them. She acted instinctively. She didn't want Lucy Killane to see that she had started packing, that she was thinking of leaving.

Not just leaving, she thought grimly. Running away! Wasn't that what she would be doing if she left now? Her mother had run away, as far as she possibly could, right across to the other side of the world—but what good had it done her? She had wasted years of her life in bitterness. Prue didn't want to do that. She had seen the consequences of brooding over a wrong done to you—you ended up doing far more damage to yourself than the original injury.

She wasn't going back to Australia, she decided then, in a flash of self-knowledge. She wasn't going to let this overshadow her whole life. Damn the Killanes! Who were they, anyway? It was time somebody taught them that they couldn't just reach out and take what they wanted, wreck other people's lives for a whim!

She had left her bedroom door slightly ajar. Lucy Killane tapped on it before pushing it wide open and looking across the room at her.

Prue stared back, sitting there immovably on her bed, her hands clasped together in her lap to stop them shaking.

'Oh, Prue,' Lucy said huskily. 'I . . . I don't know what to say to you!' She was as pale as Prue herself; her eyes had reddened lids, she had been crying. She looked drawn and haggard, and Prue couldn't help a twinge of compassion for her, because, after all, Lynsey was her daughter and only eighteen, but Prue didn't soften or show any sympathy, it would have made it harder to hang on to her self-control, so she put up a pretence of icy composure, using it as a shield.

'There's nothing useful you can say,' she told Mrs Killane. 'And I would rather you didn't say anything at all.'

'I know how you feel . . .' Mrs Killane came further into the room, and Prue frowned.

'I don't think you do, Mrs Killane! Please go, there's no point in talking about it.'

'Oh, Prue, I'm sorry, so very sorry . . .' Mrs Killane put out her hands to Prue, her lovely eyes glistening with tears, her mouth quivering. 'I'm no good with words, I don't know the right thing to say, but I feel so badly about this . . . it's terrible. How could Lynsey . . .?' Her voice was shaky and thin, it kept dying away, and then another little burst of words would burst out. 'I don't know how she could . . . We had no idea, Prue, I promise you that! Josh didn't suspect, neither did I. I couldn't believe it when he told me. He asked if I'd known, but if I had, I'd have done something to stop it, and so would Josh!'

She had seized Prue's hands and Prue couldn't quite bring herself to push her away or free herself forcibly; she had to sit there while the other woman clasped her hands, tears running freely now, down her pale, haggard, yet still hauntingly lovely face.

'She's just a child,' she sobbed. 'Just eighteen . . . she doesn't know what she's doing.'

Prue's face tightened. Oh, no? she thought, and Lucy Killane read the angry cynicism in her green eyes and flinched as if Prue had hit her.

'She's in love with love, that's all,' she whispered, as if begging Prue to agree with her. 'It can't be the real thing, she barely knows him.'

Prue laughed angrily. 'The real thing? Of course it isn't!'

Lucy looked at her with pity and anxiety, and Prue's hackles rose. She didn't want either emotion from the woman who had ruined her mother's life.

'It's just a crush, isn't it?' said Lucy, nodding. 'She's too young to know what real love is! This is because he was a stranger, from the other side of the world, and in hospital—it seemed romantic and exciting, and she mistook what she was feeling for something else! Having to keep her visits a secret probably made it twice as romantic. But I'm ashamed of her, she should have realised what it would do to you!'

'She doesn't care what she does to me!' Prue said

savagely, her green eyes flashing. She pulled her hands free and walked to the window, fighting her temper, but in the end she couldn't hold back her real feelings, they burst out of her. 'You know very well . . . she only wanted David because he belonged to me. If he had been unattached she probably wouldn't have looked twice at him, but she's your daughter, and she prefers to take her men from other women.'

Lucy Killane stood there in a frozen silence, staring at her.

'Oh, don't pretend to look bewildered,' Prue snapped. 'You don't fool me, any more than you fooled my mother!'

'She told you . . .' Lucy began, then took a deep breath. 'What? What did she tell you?'

'The truth! She thought I was old enough to know what had ruined my parents' marriage . . . or rather, who had!'

Lucy put a hand to her mouth, whitening, then a wave of red flowed up to her hairline. 'Oh, so that's why . . . why you were so offhand with me when you first arrived?'

'Until I was stupid enough to let you charm me into forgetting everything my mother had told me! But that's what you're good at—you and your daughter, and your . . . your whole damn family! You have a genius for charming people into forgetting things . . . little, unimportant things . . . like loyalty and decency and common sense!'

'But it wasn't true!' Lucy said huskily, still very flushed. 'My husband meant everything to me; I loved him very much, I never once looked at any other man. Your father and I were friends, just as he was my husband's friend. You ought to know your father better than to believe he would betray one of his oldest friends; he'd known my husband far longer than I had.'

'But you knew what I was talking about at once!' Prue said coldly, and Lucy sighed.

'Oh, your mother accused us . . . one day she came to the house and made a very unpleasant scene, shouting and crying. I was very upset, I tried to tell her the truth, but I knew that she wasn't very stable, I didn't take her seriously. Jim told me to forget it, he said she hadn't really believed the things she said, she was pathologically jealous and given to these outbursts. He said she was even jealous of his dog.' Lucy paused, face hesitant, worried, then plunged on, 'She was jealous of you, too, Prue. It drove her crazy if she thought your father loved you more than her.'

Prue's green eyes opened wide, her pupils very black. That was true; although she had forgotten it until now, she had always known her mother was jealous whenever she and her father were together. What else had she forgotten about those childhood years? she wondered, and oddly remembered Josh teasing her by saying that he had kissed her years ago. Had he lied? Ever since he had said it, some faint memory had been trying to surface; she felt it almost within reach for a second . . . then it was gone again on dragonfly wings.

Lucy was unaware of her reverie. 'And after she went away, and took you with her, Jim said she had taken you to make sure you grew up hating him,' Lucy went on, and that was true, too. Her mother

had wanted her to hate her father; that was why she
had told her so much about the past, blackening his
name. That was something Prue had worked out for
herself years ago, but her mother's jealous nature
and instability didn't mean that there was no truth to
all her wild accusations, did it? There must be some
fire behind all that smoke.

'Your two children must have got it from
somewhere, though!' Prue said bitingly, and Lucy
Killane looked dumbfounded.

'My two . . .'

'Lynsey . . . and Josh! Yes! They're as bad as each
other!'

'Josh?' repeated his mother with incredulity.

'Yes, Josh,' Prue snapped. 'I know how Lynsey
managed to seduce David, because her brother tried
the same game with me, flirting with me every time I
saw him, trying to kiss me and . . . only he didn't take
me in the way your daughter fooled poor David.'

Lucy Killane stared at her. 'Josh has been flirting
with you?' Her voice was slow, almost dazed, but
there was a thoughtful look in her face.

'Don't pretend to be shocked! I can't stand
hypocrisy!' Prue said with contempt. 'He's your son,
we both know where he got it from!'

They had been so absorbed that they hadn't heard
the creak on the stairs, and weren't aware of the
man in the doorway until he spoke, making them
jump.

'Prue!' he said sharply, and they both looked
round, startled and shaken.

Lucy Killane flushed up at the sight of him; she
turned hurriedly away, her face distressed. By

contrast, James Allardyce was white-faced and his eyes were appalled.

'Don't talk to Mrs Killane like that!' he said, and Prue laughed angrily.

'Mrs Killane? It's a bit late to be so formal, Dad. I know about you two, I've always known, Mum told me.'

Hot blood rose up in his face and he glanced quickly at Lucy Killane, who begged him, 'Tell her it isn't true, Jim!' but she couldn't look at him, all the same, and Prue read guilt in her averted eyes.

'Yes, lie to me, Dad,' Prue said. 'Tell me you don't love her!'

He looked grim, his head bent, a frown pulling his brows together. 'Your mother was sick, she invented grievances to give herself a reason for hurting me, she lied to you, Prue. There was nothing going on between me and Lucy, we were just friends. I give you my word of honour that that's the truth.' His eyes lifted and she looked into them and believed the level stare, believed even more the unhappiness, the distress, because the truth he was telling was not quite the whole truth and he knew it. She knew it, too, and was suddenly very sorry for him.

She didn't know exactly how it had been, of course. His face had a dignity which made her believe he half spoke the truth. Perhaps he hadn't been in love with Lucy Killane at first? Maybe he had simply no longer been in love with her mother and unable to counterfeit a feeling which had died? Prue knew just how difficult her mother had been; how hard to love or convince you loved her!

But, however it had come about, James Allardyce had fallen in love with Lucy Killane in the end. Perhaps when her mother accused him, she had unknowingly put the idea into his head? If he hadn't taken that sort of interest in Lucy Killane before, it would have made him see her in a new light after his wife became jealous.

Whether or not it had been true then, it was the truth now! Her father did love Lucy Killane; the silent admission was in his troubled glance, whatever he might be saying aloud, but Prue could see more than that in his eyes. Lucy did not love him and he had no hope that she ever would, except as a friend. Did Lucy know how he felt? Had she guessed long ago, or had he somehow managed to hide it from her? That Prue couldn't guess, but his eyes had a melancholy resignation; a sadness which had accepted the way things were.

Prue ran a shaking hand over her ruffled red hair, trying to think of something to say, but she couldn't get a word out except a whispered, 'Sorry, Dad.'

He knew she meant more than a simple apology for having upset Mrs Killane, but all he said, rather gruffly, was, 'Don't say that to me—say it to Mrs Killane!'

Prue turned, the words on her lips, but Lucy Killane shook her head, smiling at her wistfully.

'It's all right, Prue, no need to say it, I understand . . . she was your mother, of course you were upset. In your place, I'd have felt the same, and I'm not angry, although it wasn't true, any of it! I'm just sad for her, and for you, too. It can't have been easy for you, coping with all that while you were so young, but don't forget how sick she was. I don't suppose she knew what she was saying half the time.'

Prue gave a long sigh and nodded.

It had been a relief to her when Harry appeared and her mother married him; Harry had taken some of the weight off her own shoulders and she had been grateful to him, but her mother had never really been a happy woman and she hadn't put her bitterness behind her. She had lived with the bad memories every day, and made Prue and Harry live with them, too.

'She was sick,' Prue said, in wry forgiveness for her now, recognising how wrong she had been and yet how sad her life had been.

'I was horrified when your mother accused me,' Lucy said. 'It wasn't true, not a word of it, but when she talked about me flirting with Jim, I found myself wondering if I unwittingly ever had . . . if you smile at a man it can be misunderstood, can't it?' She gave Prue a rueful smile. 'Well, you know that, Prue! Every woman does! We all know how easy it is to give a man the wrong impression.'

Was she talking about Josh? thought Prue, high colour rushing up to her face, but Lucy went on talking in a voice which held no double meanings.

'Try to be friendly and some men will jump to the craziest conclusions, and I had a bad time for a while, wondering if I'd missed something. But Jim reassured me, he told me if was all in your mother's head, not his!' She smiled at him warmly as she added, 'That was a big relief!'

'Well, thank you!' Jim Allardyce said cheerfully and Lucy laughed.

'You know what I mean, Jim!'

'Of course I do—I was only teasing,' he said, and Lucy smiled back at him, then her face sobered again.

'With all this, I'd forgotten . . . Oh, Jim, have you heard? Such terrible news . . . Prue's fiancé . . .'

'Yes, Josh met me, he told me,' Jim Allardyce said, looking at his daughter anxiously. 'Prue darling, I'm sorry . . .'

She had herself under control now; she felt oddly lighter, as though discovering the truth about her parents had lifted a weight from her.

'Well, better that he should walk away now than after we were married,' she said lightly, her head held high, and her father's eyes searched her face for clues to what she was really feeling. Prue smiled at him defiantly.

'That's my girl!' Jim Allardyce said with the gentleness she remembered from her childhood.

'If only we knew where they had gone!' said Lucy, face bleak. 'You can't just walk in off the street and get married, even today. They would have to get a licence, make arrangements. Do you think they can be in London? Josh seems to think that's where they'd go. What do you think, Prue?'

'Maybe,' Prue said wearily, wishing they would go because she didn't want to talk about it. 'David likes London; he's a big city boy, grew up in Sydney, lived there all his life. He loves the sea; he swims like a fish and surfs whenever he can, but apart from the beach he never cared for much for the countryside; I could see he wasn't much struck by Yorkshire while we were driving up here. It was too isolated for him. He prefers bright lights and having a good time, so I wouldn't be surprised if he hasn't headed back down south to London.'

Her father grimaced. 'But where do you start looking? You can't call in the police to hunt for Lynsey. She's legally an adult, she's free to come or go as she pleases and the police won't want to know.'

'I think Josh is considering getting a private detective,' Lucy told him.

'Josh ought to let it go. It'll be like looking for a needle in a haystack!' said Jim Allardyce bluntly.

Lucy groaned, moving restlessly towards the door. 'Shall we go downstairs and have some tea while we talk? I'm dying of thirst, aren't you, Prue? All this agitation makes one thirsty, don't you think?'

Jim Allardyce followed her, but Prue was reluctant to talk any more.

'You know,' said Lucy, over her shoulder, 'what I still can't believe is how Lynsey could act that way. Sneaking into that hospital every day, secretly visiting a strange young man she knows is engaged to someone else! I didn't know my own daughter, did I? Did anyone? I've never seen Josh so angry, he's like a thunderstorm in the house.'

Prue sat down on the bed abruptly, her knees too weak to hold her up any longer. When Lucy talked about Josh she almost saw him; that dark, angry face, those glittering eyes flashing at her—the mere idea of him made her stomach cave in and her heart crash against her ribs.

His mother had hit the nail right on the head when

she said that he was like a thunderstorm in the
house. That was just what Josh was . . . an elemental
creature of darkness and storm!

'Are you OK?' Her father stood beside her, looking
down into her pale face with anxiety.

'Yes, I'm just . . . tired,' she lied.

'Tired,' he repeated, frowning, and Lucy turned
back into the room, her face guilty.

'Oh, poor Prue, you do look tired. You've had a
shock, you should be resting. Lie down on your bed
and I'll come up with a tray in a minute. Something
light, an omelette, a glass of milk?'

'No, nothing!' Prue said, and heard the sharpness
in her own voice, sighing. 'Sorry, I didn't mean to
snap, it's just that I'm not hungry and I'd like to have
an hour or two on my own.'

'Of course,' they said, and tiptoed out as if she was
a child. The door closed and Prue lay back on the bed,
staring up at the ceiling. She had often lain in this
room during those long ago childhood years,
listening to the wind blowing over the moors, the cry
of birds, the distant barking of a fox somewhere on
the hill, or the angry voices of the adults downstairs.
She shut her eyes and it came back vividly; that
feeling of helplessness and misery.

She tried to think of something happier; she
deliberately conjured up memories of running
through the fields on a warm summer morning
watching the larks high up above; suspended in mid-
heaven and singing like angels.

She must have drifted off to sleep soon afterwards,
because she dreamt of being at a party, a children's
party at Killane House. Prue was wandering through

the maze of passages and rooms; frightened by the boom of the wind in the chimneys, wondering where everyone else had vanished. They were playing some childish game; hide and seek, maybe. She heard a sound in a cupboard and opened it; it was dark inside but somebody moved in the darkness, somebody's hand reached out and grabbed her, dragged her into the cupboard, slamming the door behind her before she could escape again.

'Got you!' somebody whispered, and Prue screamed, high and shrill, but before she could scream again somebody kissed her.

She had never been kissed like that before; his mouth was warm and moist, it tasted of cider, which some of the older boys at the party had been drinking. Prue was too startled to kiss him back or to fight him off; she just stood there, wide-eyed and breathless.

'Who . . .?' she whispered, unable to see his face in the dark little space.

'Who? Twit twoo . . .' he mocked, and then suddenly pushed her out of the cupboard again just as a little crowd of her friends ran past. Prue was carried along with them and the dream dissolved into another dream of being chased across the moors by someone she couldn't see, someone who terrified her.

'Wake up,' someone said, far away, and she tossed and turned.

'No, leave me alone.'

'Wake up,' the deep voice said again, nearer now, and then she was back in the dark cupboard, his mouth closing over hers, warm and hard, the contours of it familiar yet strange; and Prue jackknifed upwards, gasping and panic-stricken.

'No!'

Her eyes flew open and she looked into Josh's face with a sense of terror; yet she had known it was Josh before she looked, she had known all the time; she had known in the dark little cupboard in her dream—but why had she dreamt that she was a child?

'You were having a nightmare,' he said. 'You wouldn't wake up when I called you.'

He was on the bed, leaning over her; too close, much too close. She stared into his eyes and saw that their darkness had golden centres; little rays of gold around the glittering black pupil. His lashes were thicker than she had realised, too, and as she stared at him he drooped the lashes over his eyes as if hiding something from her.

'Where's my father?' she asked huskily.

'He went back to work.' Josh ran a lazy hand over her tousled hair and she shivered.

'Don't do that!' She swung her legs off the bed and picked up a brush from the dressing-table, began brushing her hair with rough strokes.

Conscious of Josh watching her, she asked flatly, 'Any news?'

'Of them? No,' he said, his face grim. 'I've been to see a detective agency in York. They have contacts all over the country, but they don't hold out much hope of finding them with so little to go on. It would help if we got a letter from them, or they applied for a marriage licence somewhere, but the chances of our catching up with them are slim.'

She brushed automatically, frowning. 'I still think

your sister will leave him after a few days.'

'Wishful thinking,' he drawled, his face sardonic. 'You still haven't told me . . if she did leave him, would you want him back?'

She didn't answer him. He had been to York while she slept? It was twilight; the room was full of shadows. She must have slept for hours, but she didn't feel refreshed, her body was languid and her mind in turmoil. The shock of David's letter had bowled her over—or was it only that? She had been increasingly on edge for days, and she knew it. She knew who had caused her uneasiness, too, and she looked in the mirror at him, her green eyes resentful.

'What are you doing in my room, anyway?' she asked Josh angrily, and he lay back on her rumpled bed, his long body lazily at ease, his hands behind his head and his face mocking as he watched her.

'Waking you up, Sleeping Beauty. The traditional way; with a kiss. You've been asleep for hours; I promised your father I'd look in to see that you were OK, but when I came up here I heard you talking in your sleep and it sounded as if you were having a bad nightmare. Do you remember what it was all about?'

'No,' she said shortly, eyeing herself in the dressing-table mirror and furious at the way she looked. Her shirt and jeans were creased. She was a mess.

'Was I in it?' he asked, grinning.

'Yes,' she said, to wipe the self-satisfaction out of his face.

But he just laughed. 'I walked into that one, didn't I?'

'Look,' Prue said, 'I want to change my clothes. Please go.'

He considered her with that lazy grin. 'Wear that green sweater you wore the other day. It makes your figure very sexy.'

Her eyes flashed; she went pink with temper. She marched across the room, opened the door wide. 'Goodbye, Mr Killane. I'll be OK, thank you, there's no need to stay.'

He casually got up, sauntered towards her, but didn't go, just stood there looking down at her, his brows arched.

'You're well rid of him, you know,' he said suddenly, and Prue's flush became hotter.

'I'm not discussing David with you!'

'You've known him for years, haven't you?'

'Goodbye, Mr Killane!'

'You got engaged over a year ago, you told me so yourself—but neither of you felt any urgency about getting married. Doesn't that tell you something?'

'Will you shut up?' she blazed, her green eyes glittering like ice emerald. He had been needling her long enough; she was sick of it. He had started getting at her almost from the very first. She should have kept out of his way; she couldn't help feeling that he was behind everything that had happened, he had caused it.

'It's all your fault, anyway!' she accused.

'I suppose I might have known it would turn out to be,' he said drily. 'But tell me how, just for the sake of curiosity?'

She looked helplessly at him, trying to justify the charge, and remembered something she had forgotten until that moment.

'That day your sister walked in and saw us!' she slowly said, eyes widening. 'Yes, I see it now . . . she jumped to all sorts of conclusions . . .'

'Some of them very accurate,' he intervened, grinning, and she scowled at him.

'All of them wrong! You were making a pass at me! I wasn't encouraging you!'

'No?' he drawled, and her teeth met.

She took a long breath, then said sharply, 'I'm ready to bet she went straight off to tell David something was going on between you and me, and that's why David thought I wouldn't care whether he went or not.'

'For once Lynsey wasn't far wrong, though, was she?' Josh said.

'Lynsey jumped at her chance,' Prue thought aloud, ignoring what he'd said. 'Maybe the two of you set it up beforehand? Planned for her to walk in just then so that she could go to David and tell him . . .'

'Don't be ridiculous!' Josh had stopped looking amused, he was angry, then he smoothed out his frown and gave her a wry look. 'Stop fooling yourself, Prue. I watched you with him in the hospital that day Lynsey went back to give him flowers—the two of you acted like friends, not lovers!'

'You don't know either of us . . .' she burst out in a hoarse voice.

'I know you,' Josh said softly, standing very close

to her, his eyes pure provocation. 'I know you intimately, Prue, although not as intimately as I'd like.'

She drew a sharp breath. 'And you never will!' she hissed, and he smiled in that mocking, lazy way, nodding.

'Oh, yes!'

'Don't kid yourself! You won't, not ever . . .' But she was shaking from head to foot, because his body exerted a magnetism which drew her like a needle seeking the north, quivering involuntarily and turning in a helpless obedience, and his dark eyes told her that he knew what happened whenever she was near him.

'Losing him isn't going to wreck your life, is it?' Josh murmured, his gaze intent on her face. 'You aren't broken-hearted, Prue, don't pretend you are.'

'Get out!' she muttered. 'I hate you. Stop talking about it, leave me alone. I can't stand you near me.'

She got home to him with that; she felt his body tense, saw his eyes narrow and flash. 'Isn't that too bad?' he said harshly. 'Well, you're going to have to stand it, right now . . .' He reached for her and she went into panic again and hit out at him with closed fists, yelling.

'Don't touch me . . . I'm not staying here, I'm going tomorrow . . . back to Australia . . .'

Josh froze, staring at her. For a long moment they looked at each other from across an abyss, then Josh snarled at her, 'Go, then, damn you to hell—go to Australia and never come back!' He turned on his heel and went, crashing down the stairs and out of the front door, leaving her numb.

CHAPTER NINE

SHE hadn't meant to go, she didn't want to return to Australia, and the last thing on her mind was to continue with her holiday trip to Europe, but her quarrel with Josh had changed everything. His last words kept echoing inside her head and she listened to them in that frozen stillness, icy with shock.

Go away, go back to Australia, damn you! he'd told her as if he hated her—and Prue sat on her bed, with a white face and eyes dark with pain, facing something she had been trying to avoid admitting ever since she first set eyes on Josh Killane.

She didn't hate him at all; she had been lying to herself like crazy and it had to stop now. The admission was painful; her mouth went dry, her body trembled, her nerve-ends quivered as if at the touch of fire on her skin, but she made herself face it.

She was in love with Josh, and it was nothing like the warm, happy, casual feeling she had had with David. David had never made her feel like this; she hadn't even known it was possible to want someone with this bitter intensity, but from the moment she saw Josh that was how she had felt and that was why she had hated him, quarrelled with him, resented him.

Her feelings had scared her! She hadn't known how to cope with that agonising ache of aroused sensuality, except by converting desire into rage because it hid her real emotions from Josh as well as herself, but now she would no longer be able to go on pretending. The secret was out of her unconscious and now it would be ten times harder to hide it from Josh.

She was bound to give herself away sooner or later, and once Josh knew how she felt, he would put pressure on her; he would talk her into bed and Prue would hate herself if she let him. She might love Josh, but he wasn't the type to take a woman seriously. He had flirted with her, even though he knew she was engaged to marry another man—Josh didn't believe in love, he was opportunist, a sexual pirate, a disastrous man to love.

She got off the bed and slowly began to pack again. She couldn't stay here now. She had to get away. She would go up to London first, to give herself time to decide what she really wanted to do. Maybe she would get a job in London? Or perhaps she would be safer back in Australia?

She couldn't think clearly; she didn't know where to go yet and her mind was in such a muddle that she gave up trying to decide—only one thing seemed crystal-clear to her. She had to get away; now, at once.

She flung clothes into her cases and locked them, then she had a shower and put on a freshly ironed shirt and a clean pair of jeans. She couldn't drive all the way down England in crumpled clothes. She did something about her make-up, looked at herself

wryly in the dressing-table mirror, recognising that
she might now be neat in appearance but she still
looked tense and edgy. There was nothing she could
do about that, so she went downstairs with her
cases.

The farmhouse seemed oddly empty; she wished
her father was there so that she could say goodbye to
him, but if he had been around she knew he would
have tried to talk her out of going, so it was probably
just as well.

She sat down to write to him, but it was very hard
to explain why she was going without seeing him
first. She sat staring at the paper for ages, chewing
her lower lip and sighing, then she hurriedly
scribbled a brief note, saying she was sorry, she had
to go, but promising to write again soon and let him
know her address, then she put her suitcases into the
hire car and set off in the vague direction of London.
It wouldn't be hard to get a hotel room somewhere in
the city. Maybe tomorrow she would have made up
her mind what she wanted to do.

A bitter little smile curled her mouth and she
shuddered. She knew what she wanted to do now!
But she couldn't give in to the way she felt; she'd
despise herself for the rest of her life if she did. This
terrible ache of desire would ease once she was far
away from Josh; she clung on to that thought, driving
very fast, barely noticing the other traffic on the
road.

She certainly didn't notice the big, black car which
flashed past her several miles from the farm—or
rather, she didn't notice it until it did a sudden
U-turn in the middle of the road, scaring the life

out of Prue when she found herself heading straight for the other vehicle at about seventy miles an hour.

She slammed on the brakes, her tyres screamed, her car zigzagged all over the road, completely out of control, ending up off the road on a grassy verge.

Prue was thrown forward over the wheel and lay there, winded for a moment, too shattered to be aware of anything.

The driver of the black car got out and ran to open her door, she dimly felt his hands unbuckle her seat-belt, and stirred, lifting her head.

'Josh!' She hadn't recognised the other car or known who was driving it. Shock made her shake violently.

He didn't answer; he was too busy dragging her out of her car as if she was a limp doll. His hands brushed across her shirt and to her horror she felt her nipples hardening; her breasts swelling under her thin shirt. She was appalled by her own fierce reactions, and angrily turned on him. 'What the hell did you think you were doing, making a U-turn on a main road? This is the second time you've had a damn good try at killing me! Last time you blamed David—what's your excuse this time?'

'I had to stop you.'

She looked at him incredulously. 'You . . . are you saying you meant to make me crash? You're crazier than I thought! What if my brakes had failed? What if I hadn't been able to stop in time?'

'I would have reversed out of the way before you hit me,' he said, his hand an iron bracelet around her wrist.

'I've a good mind to call the police and have you charged with dangerous driving!' she fumed, trying to break free. 'I should have had you charged last time. Next time you may kill me, you reckless madman!'

Josh thrust her into his car and leaned down to say tersely, 'Last time it was Henley's fault and you know it. That was a stupid accident; this was deliberate, I just got the idea from him.' He slammed the door on her and she reached for the handle in a hurry, but Josh was faster. He got into the driver's seat and yanked her hands down.

'Keep still or I'll slap you!'

'You wouldn't dare!' she raged childishly.

His mouth curled. 'Try me.'

Prue looked into the glittering dark eyes and decided not to put him to the test.

He smiled derisively. 'Very wise!'

Prue's teeth met; she looked at him with hostility.

'Please let me out of here!' she demanded. 'I'm on my way to London.'

'I thought you might be on your way somewhere,' Josh said, his voice hard. 'That's why I stopped you. You aren't going.'

'You told me to go!' snapped Prue. 'Just a couple of hours ago you told me to go back to Australia.'

He looked at her in silence, his mouth twisting and his dark eyes intent, then sighed.

'I didn't mean it—you must know I didn't, Prue. I lost my temper and said the first thing that came into my head. I'm sorry.'

She was afraid to soften, because any weakness

towards him could be catastrophic, so she just scowled.

'Well, I'm going, anyway,' she muttered, looking down, her lashes cloaking her disturbed eyes. When he looked at her like that it made her stomach clench and her body grow languid with desire, but she mustn't let him get to her. She had to get away from him before he realised just how badly she wanted him.

'Don't,' he whispered, and moved before she had notice of his intention. His lips skated over her throat and she shivered helplessly.

'Don't do that!' Her voice sounded shaky even to her own ears, and Josh wouldn't miss the uneven note in it.

He didn't stop kissing her neck, either. He was breathing rapidly, his hands moving in a soft exploration of her imprisoned body, cupping her breasts in the thin shirt, his fingers stroking, fondling; and although she tried to fight him off, Prue inwardly ached with frustration. Her own need was growing like a forest fire; she wanted to touch him, too, to give in to the hunger she felt. It was a relief when he lifted his head again.

She spat fury at him, hoping she was convincing. 'Get your hands off me!'

She saw him flinch, his eyes as black as hell, the bones of his face tightly constricted. 'You aren't still hankering after that fool who dumped you to run off with my sister?' he bit out, glaring back. 'Don't waste your time on him, Prue, he doesn't love you, he never did!'

'What would you know about love?' she sneered,

hurt and angry at the same time. When Josh looked at her with such contempt she wanted to burst into tears, but she held her head up and tried to inject an answering dislike into her eyes.

He laughed shortly. 'More than you do, anyway!'

'I doubt it!' Prue said bitterly.

At that moment another car, passing them, slowed down, and the driver put his head out to shout, 'Hello, need any help?'

Josh sat up, darkly flushed. He leaned over to shake his head. 'No, thanks.'

'Anybody hurt in the crash?' asked the other man curiously, looking past Josh at Prue.

'No, it wasn't serious,' Josh said. 'Just a skid.'

The other man looked back at Prue's car. 'Whoever was driving that was damn lucky then! Could have been killed, veering off the road like that!' He drove on and Josh gave an ironic grimace.

'He thought I was giving you the kiss of life, I suppose.'

Prue was scarlet and unamused. 'He was right about me being lucky not to be killed!' She put a hand to the door-handle. 'Will you help me to get my car back on to the road?' she stiffly asked.

'I'd never manage it; after all the rain we've been having, that verge is much too soft. We'd just churn up the mud and probably make matters worse. Leave it there and I'll ask my garage to send someone out here to pick it up.'

Prue seethed, but there was nothing she could do but accept the situation. 'My cases are in it,' she said coldly, and Josh went over to get her suitcases and load them into his own car.

'I'll take you home,' he then said, and there was nothing much she could do about that either, not that it made her any happier to admit it.

'Will you stop trying to run my life?' she snapped as Josh started the car and began to drive away.

He stared straight ahead, both hands on the wheel, his mouth tight, his profile as sharp as a razor. 'Somebody has to!' he muttered without looking at her.

'I've managed it myself for years!' Prue bit back, scowling.

'You don't seem to have made much of a job of it so far,' Josh told her. 'You picked the most God-awful man and you jump to the craziest of conclusions about things without really knowing what you're doing!'

She opened her mouth to yell back at him, then remembered how wrong she had been about his mother, what flimsy evidence she had had for the false conclusions she had drawn about Lucy Killane—and closed her mouth again.

Josh had been watching her sideways, waiting for her come-back, and his brows lifted at her silence. 'Well, well . . . nothing to say?' he mocked, his eyes gleaming with curiosity.

'I've decided I won't let you drag me into another stupid, pointless argument; you may enjoy them, but I don't! I hate them. I've never quarrelled with anyone the way I quarrel with you, and I don't know why we keep shouting at each other . . .'

'Don't you?' he interrupted, smiling crookedly. 'I

could tell you, but . . .'

'I'm not listening!' Prue broke out, in a panic, her skin filmed with fine sweat.

'But you won't want to hear!' Josh finished drily. His smile made her face burn, then she realised that he was not taking her home, he was heading in the direction of Killane House, and she sat up rigidly.

'Where are you taking me?'

He shot her one of his dry glances. 'Where do you think?'

'I want to go back to my father's farm.'

'Later,' Josh said coolly.

'No, now! Take me home!'

He turned into the drive of Killane House without taking any notice; his profile radiated obstinacy, and she eyed him sideways with a mixture of fury and desire which was explosive, making her feel she might blow up at any minute. What did you do with a man like Josh Killane?

'You're driving me crazy,' she muttered, barely audibly.

'Snap!' he said, pulling up outside his home, then turned with his arm resting on the wheel to look down at her, his face taut with passion.

'Prue, will you please stop arguing with me for a couple of hours, just long enough to have dinner with us? My mother feels very badly about what's happened. She likes you a lot. Will you be nice to her this evening, show her you don't blame her?' His eyes were serious. 'You don't, do you?'

She shook her head, her mouth twisting. 'I suppose not, and I like your mother, too. I'm glad she likes me.'

'Is it a deal, then?'

She looked into his dark eyes and sighed, nodding.

It was a quiet evening; there were only four of them for dinner—Lucy and Josh, Prue and her father. After the beautifully cooked meal, they sat talking for several hours around a roaring fire, just one fringed lamp switched on, and black shadows leaping up to the ceiling now and again from the flames shooting out of the sweet-scented resinated pine wood. Prue drove home with her father; exhaustion and good wine combined made her sleep heavily, and she woke up to hear sounds outside, cars pulling up in front of the farmhouse, voices talking cheerfully.

Josh and a mechanic had brought her car back. She leapt out of bed, showered, dressed and went downstairs to find Josh in the kitchen drinking coffee and talking to her father. When Prue appeared, Josh looked round at her, his eyes wandering from her burnished head to her feet, mockingly assessing the bits in between and making her go pink.

'Well, up at last?' he teased.

Prue looked at her watch. 'It isn't that late! Only just nine-thirty, or has my watch stopped?'

'No,' said her father, pouring her a cup of coffee. 'Do you want some breakfast? Egg? Bacon?'

'I'll just have coffee, thanks,' she said, sitting down on the other side of the table from Josh, but smiling shyly at him. 'I see you've brought my car back. That was very good of you, thank you.'

'It was my fault you skidded off the road,' he shrugged casually. 'I got my garage to wash it before we brought it here. It needed it, believe me! It was covered in mud from where the wheels had churned up the verge while we were trying to shift it.'

'That was very thoughtful, thank you,' said Prue, very self-conscious as she felt her father watching them. Did anyone else realise how she felt about Josh? Did it show, when she looked at him? Or in her voice? Once the thought had occurred to her, she immediately began to feel horribly obvious, and to flush.

Josh got up. 'I must go, I'll be seeing you both.' He vanished and Prue sat staring at nothing, feeling lonely now that he had gone. That thought appalled her—was she becoming dependent on him so soon? That was dangerous; she must put a stop to that!

'Prue!' her father murmured, and she looked hurriedly at him, picking up his uneasiness and becoming nervous herself.

'Yes?'

'I was wondering . . . I have a mound of paperwork waiting to be dealt with, and I'd be very grateful for some help, if you wouldn't mind? I've got so much else to get through and . . .'

She laughed, her face affectionate. 'Of course I'd be glad to help, Dad. How about now, this morning?'

'That would be wonderful,' James Allardyce said with a sigh of relief. His expression eased her mind of the only doubt she had had—that he might have made up some phoney job which didn't really need doing, and when she actually saw the old desk piled high with forms, letters, government leaflets and official documents, she was quite sure that her father needed her. He needed a secretary badly, and Prue was a good secretary.

'Leave all this to me, I'll sort it out,' she said confidently, and after a token protest her father obeyed her gratefully.

She spent the next few days working her way through the long neglected office work. James Allardyce's business life was in a complex muddle, and Prue wondered how he had managed to carry on for so long with so many unanswered letters, unpaid bills, not to mention money owing to him in his turn. While he was out on his land—working with the animals, keeping his land in order, his walls mended, his trees in good shape—he had ignored everything else, but Prue gradually tidied up the office and got all the necessary work done. Letters were answered, typed out and posted; bills sent out and bills paid. Everything else was neatly filed where Prue could put her hand on it quickly.

Josh called in most days for some reason or another. He was, after all, her father's landlord, and their working lives intermeshed far more than Prue had ever suspected. He never stayed long, though, and he and Prue were never alone; James Allardyce or Betty Cain or Josh's mother were always there, which made it both easier and harder for Prue. She was relieved not to have the strain of being alone with Josh, but it didn't ease the ache of desire she felt whenever she saw him; just made it easier to hide, at least from others. She wasn't too optimistic of hiding it from Josh. His quick, shrewd, dark eyes didn't miss anything, and the occasional glance or mocking smile told her how little she fooled him, but Josh was being careful to keep his distance at the moment.

She told herself she was glad about that; she didn't want him any nearer. Somehow she didn't convince herself of her indifference to him any more than she apparently convinced Josh.

It was over a week before any news was heard of Lynsey and David, and the intervening time passed more quickly than Prue would ever have believed it could, because she was able to stop herself thinking too much by working hard. She had finished the accumulation of years of paperwork, and had begun to help her father in other ways—cooking his meals, helping him on the farm. Days began very early, and she was usually in bed and fast asleep from sheer physical exhaustion by ten-thirty.

She was busy preparing a casserole for her father's supper one afternoon when Josh walked in without knocking. Her heart turned over as she looked round.

'Oh, it's you!' she said huskily. It was the first time she had seen him for two days and she was very conscious of the empty house around them. 'Dad's tramping the fields. If you want him you could catch him at . . .'

'No, I want you,' Josh said, and Prue swallowed, her eyes lowered.

'Oh?'

'We've heard from them.'

'From who?' she blankly asked, and then looked up, turning pale. 'Oh . . . David?'

'And Lynsey,' said Josh flatly, his brows black above his watchful eyes. 'We had a letter this morning.'

Prue looked down again at the steak she was cutting up, trying to hide a dismay she felt at the thought of news from the runaways. She didn't know how she would cope if David and Lynsey had parted, or if David came back here and she had to face him. He had walked out on her, so he probably wouldn't dare ask her to take him back, but if he did she would have to say no and David would think it was jealousy. But did it matter what he thought?

'Well?' she asked huskily when Josh didn't immediately tell her what the letter had said. 'What did David say? Where is he?'

'They're married, and in another week they'll be on their way to Australia,' Josh curtly told her, sounding so savage that her hand slipped, and instead of cutting the steak the sharp, serrated knife cut her finger, and she gave a sharp gasp, dropping the knife. Blood welled up on her skin and she put the finger to her mouth, the pain bringing a glaze of unshed tears to her eyes.

'What have you done?' Josh asked harshly, taking hold of her hand and making her show him the cut finger.

'It's nothing,' she muttered, shaking at his touch, and he gave her a bleak stare.

'Is that why you're crying and trembling like a leaf? Over nothing?'

Prue bit her lip. 'Don't . . .' she whispered, trying to turn away, but he wouldn't let go of her, his hands cruel, gripping her elbows and shaking her violently.

'Don't what? Tell you the truth? No, you wouldn't want to hear that, would you? It would blow apart the cosy little fantasy you prefer to real life, and that would never do!'

The tears slipped from under her lids, trickling down her pale face. 'Why are you shouting at me? It isn't my fault your sister ran off with David and married him!'

'It's your fault you're crying over him,' Josh snarled. He tightened his grip on her arms, jerked her towards him and kissed her ruthlessly, his mouth hot and angry. 'I ought to kiss you until you start seeing straight,' he muttered against her quivering mouth, and kissed her again so hard that she couldn't breathe.

Prue was too distraught to fight; she closed her eyes and her lips parted moistly, kissing him back, her body swaying against him. Josh let go of her arms and slid his hands around her waist, one hand moving convulsively up and down her spine, pressing her closer and closer until their bodies were moulded together. She flung her arms round his neck and clutched at his hair, twisting warm strands of it around her fingers.

He lifted his head, breathing fast, and looked at her through half-closed lids, dark eyes gleaming. 'When are you going to face it?' he asked and Prue moaned, looking back at him helplessly.

'Josh . . .'

'You don't love Henley, you never did,' he insisted, and she sighed admission.

'I thought I did.'

His eyes flashed. 'But you know better now.'

'I'm not the type to be able to have light affairs,' Prue whispered, her green eyes glittering with tears.

'I can't flirt with every man I meet, or go to bed with someone then forget them next day!'

His brows rose and a sardonic amusement lit his face. 'My God, I'm glad to hear it—neither am I.'

She stared back. 'But . . . you are, that's just it! From the minute we met, you flirted, kissed me, made passes, and we were total strangers!'

'Not exactly,' he said. 'I'd known you from the day you were born until you were thirteen—that doesn't make you a stranger.'

'We hardly ever met then! You were already grown up. I don't think we exchanged two words.'

'We kissed,' he said, the sardonic glimmer stronger.

She frowned. 'You said that before, but I don't remember ever kissing you!'

He laughed. 'We had a Christmas party up at Killane House, for Lynsey, not me—all the children living on the estate, all our tenants' children, and friends of Lynsey's from school. We gave them tea and organised the usual games kids love: murder in the dark, charades.'

Prue was very still, remembering her strange dream. 'I was there, wasn't I?'

His dark eyes mocked. 'Oh, you were there, sweetheart. You were wearing a very pretty dress, I remember—very simple white organdie in the Regency style, high-waisted, with a long, straight skirt and a little round neckline, a green velvet sash round your waist. You looked charming, with that red hair of yours hanging down in ringlets. You suddenly didn't look like a little girl, any more. It was obvious you were going to be a beautiful woman before too long.'

Prue was disturbed; she could remember her dream of the other night but she couldn't remember the party, which was odd. Flushed and uncertain, she watched Josh, and he looked back at her searchingly, hunting in her face for the memory he wanted.

'One of the games we all played was hide and seek,' he said, eyes narrowed, and Prue took a sharp breath. 'Yes?' asked Josh, but she shook her head.

'I didn't say anything.'

'I thought you were going to—never mind,' he said. 'I hid in a cupboard up in the attic and after a while the door opened and . . .'

'Oh,' Prue broke out, trembling, and he put a hand to her face, stroking her cheek, his index finger softly following the line of her mouth.

'Yes, you were there, and I pulled you into the cupboard and kissed you.'

How had she forgotten it for so long? she wondered. Had it been such a traumatic shock that she had wiped out the memory rather than face up to what it meant?

Josh grimaced. 'Then a whole lot of other people came past and you ran after them, and I stayed in the cupboard, feeling pretty stupid. I was almost twice your age, you were just a kid, a little girl of thirteen—and I was in my twenties! I didn't know what had come over me, except that you looked so different that night, you were lovely, and I'd been staring at you all through the party, thinking how you were growing up, and how gorgeous you were going to be.' He cupped her chin with his palm, tilting her head back so that she was looking up at him. 'You do remember, don't you? Did I scare the living daylights out of you?'

'No,' she said slowly, her green eyes thoughtful. 'It was what happened the next day, I think.'

He looked baffled. 'What happened the next day? I don't remember anything.'

'My mother burst out with all her jealousy of your mother—she hated the Killanes, and I . . .'

Shrewdly he finished for her, 'Felt guilty because you had let a Killane kiss you?'

She nodded, mouth wry. 'I didn't remember the party or that you had kissed me, you know—I do remember it now that you've reminded me, but until this minute I seem to have suppressed the whole incident, maybe because I was afraid that if she found out, my mother would hate me too?' She thought for a moment, then added huskily, 'Especially . . .' Her voice broke off and she swallowed, her face dusky pink.

'Especially?' queried Josh, arching his brows, but she didn't answer, and after a moment he softly suggested, 'Especially as you'd liked it when I kissed you?'

She looked down, half smiling, but didn't answer. She had already admitted too much.

'I wonder if that's why you were so virulently against my whole family, but especially me, when you came back here?' Josh thought aloud. 'It wasn't just your mother that had made you see us all in the role of seducers and flirts. I'd helped to give you that impression, even if you were suppressing the memory.' He laughed shortly. 'I was my own enemy without realising it!'

'Possibly,' Prue said a little sadly. 'We're all our own worst enemies, aren't we?' Why had she dreamt about that party, the kiss, except that her own subconscious had been trying to tell her how she really felt about Josh? She had dreamt she was a child, and in emotional terms she was still half childish—that was why she had fixed on David for a life partner, because he didn't come anywhere near touching her at that deepest part of her emotions. She was fond of David, she liked him, but she would never have loved him with the intensity she felt for Josh—she had chosen David because he was safe and would never hurt her.

'At least I never forgot you!' Josh said drily. 'Far from suppressing the memory of kissing you that day, I kept remembering it year after year. I wouldn't go so far as to say that that was why I never married, but I think that at the back of my head I had this image of the girl I was looking for and none of them matched up to her.' His dark eyes glimmered with passion and mockery. 'None of them had the right shade of red hair or the right slanty green eyes!'

Her breath caught.

'I love you, Prue,' he whispered, then waited, and Prue shook, fighting a last-ditch battle with her fear and her uncertainty, then she whispered it back.

'I love you.'

'Ah . . .' he breathed, closing his eyes, and his face glowed with triumph; then he opened his eyes and looked at her with an unleashed passion that sent the blood singing through her veins. Josh bent his head, and she met his mouth with all the desire she had been hiding for so long, knowing that she need never hide her feelings again.

Harlequin Presents

Coming Next Month

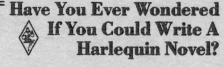

Have You Ever Wondered If You Could Write A Harlequin Novel?

Here's great news—Harlequin is offering a series of cassette tapes to help you do just that. Written by Harlequin editors, these tapes give practical advice on how to make your characters—and your story— come alive. There's a tape for each contemporary romance series Harlequin publishes.

Mail order only

All sales final

TO: ***Harlequin Reader Service***
Audiocassette Tape Offer
P.O. Box 1396
Buffalo, NY 14269-1396

I enclose a check/money order payable to HARLEQUIN READER SERVICE® for $9.70 ($8.95 plus 75¢ postage and handling) for EACH tape ordered for the total sum of $_____*
Please send:

☐ Romance and Presents   ☐ Intrigue
☐ American Romance   ☐ Temptation
☐ Superromance   ☐ All five tapes ($38.80 total)

Signature_____
                               (please print clearly)
Name:_____
Address:_____
State:_____ Zip:_____

*Iowa and New York residents add appropriate sales tax.

AUDIO-H

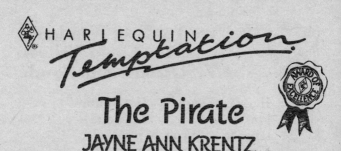

The Pirate
JAYNE ANN KRENTZ

At the heart of every powerful romance story lies a legend. There are many romantic legends and countless modern variations on them, but they all have one thing in common: They are tales of brave, resourceful women who must gentle and tame the powerful, passionate men who are their true mates.

The enormous appeal of Jayne Ann Krentz lies in her ability to create modern-day versions of these classic romantic myths, and her LADIES AND LEGENDS trilogy showcases this talent. Believing that a storyteller who can bring legends to life deserves special attention, Harlequin has chosen the first book of the trilogy—THE PIRATE—to receive our Award of Excellence. Look for it in February.

AE-PIR-1

Harlequin Superromance®

LET THE GOOD TIMES ROLL...

Add some Cajun spice to liven up your New Year's celebrations and join Superromance for a romantic tour of the rich Acadian marshlands and the legendary Louisiana bayous.

Starting in January 1990, we're launching CAJUN MELODIES, a three-book tribute to the fun-loving people who've enriched America by introducing us to crawfish étouffé and gumbo, zydeco music and the Saturday night party, the *fais-dodo*. And learn about loving, Cajun-style, as you meet the tall, dark, handsome men who win their ladies' hearts with a beautiful, haunting melody....

Book One: *Julianne's Song*, January 1990
Book Two: *Catherine's Song*, February 1990
Book Three: *Jessica's Song*, March 1990

A compelling novel of deadly revenge and passion from Harlequin's bestselling international romance author Penny Jordan

Eleven years had passed but the terror of that night was something Pepper Minesse would never forget. Fueled by revenge against the four men who had brutally shattered her past, she set in motion a deadly plan to destroy their futures.

Available in February!

HPP-1A